JOLTS

FERNANDO SDRIGOTTI

Published by Influx Press
The Greenhouse
49 Green Lanes, London, N16 9BU
www.influxpress.com / @InfluxPress
All rights reserved.
© Fernando Sdrigotti, 2020

Copyright of the text rests with the author.

The right of Fernando Sdrigotti to be identified as the author of this work has been asserted in accordance with section 77 of the Copyright, Designs and Patents Act 1988.

This book is in copyright. Subject to statutory exception and to provisions of relevant collective licensing agreements, no reproduction of any part may take place without the written permission of Influx Press.

First edition 2020.
Printed and bound in the UK by TJ International.

Paperback ISBN: 9781910312513
Ebook ISBN: 9781910312520

Editor: Kit Caless
Assistant Editor: Sanya Semakula
Cover design: Austin Burke
Interior design: Vince Haig

This book is sold subject to the condition that it shall not, by way of trade or otherwise, be lent, re-sold, hired out, or otherwise circulated without the publisher's prior consent in any form of binding or cover other than that in which it is published and without a similar condition including this condition being imposed on the subsequent purchaser.

CONTENTS

JoLTS

If they don't see happiness in the picture,
at least they'll see the black.
CHRIS MARKER

Undated

A packed unmoving train in Clapham Junction. What happened before is beyond the point — this train could be everything there is to this world. A packed train where the air stinks of café latte and where the passengers are starting to tut and puff in their winter coats and jackets. Faces, one after the other, all bleary-eyed and lethargic.

8:33 a.m., December 12, 2014

He's reading the news on his iPad, learning that some celebrity he doesn't know has left the jungle on a TV show he doesn't watch. His train is delayed or cancelled — all trains are, because of the snow. But what really bothers him this morning is the guy who was listening to his music without headphones on the 341 bus from Angel Road Superstores to

Waterloo. The guy was listening to Nirvana and suddenly twenty years passed since Nirvana, one after the other, on that 341 bus. It's not about Nirvana, of course: it's about time and about him being out of synch with himself.

3:13 a.m., December 13, 1999

I'm walking with Walter when we bump into Julio on the corner of Corrientes and Tucumán, Rosario. Julio is pissing against a wall, off his head, talking to himself, almost falling with his pants all the way down to his ankles and a tetrapack of wine in his left hand. It's a hot and humid summer night and it will rain — mixing glue with wine is a bad idea on nights like these. He finishes pissing and turns around and comes our way, still with his pants down, hopping like a kangaroo, until he pulls them up. He's wearing his Nirvana tee, the same one he's been wearing since 1995, and doesn't recognise me. He tries to mug me. I grab him by the neck and tell him, 'Julio, you cunt, it's me.' He smiles: two of his front teeth are missing. He gets a piece of paper from his pocket and tells me, 'Look, it came back negative,' as if it was the most normal thing to say. The paper looks dodgy and people have been saying he's got AIDS for a while, but he might as well be negative for all I care. He doesn't apologise for trying to rob me and walks away and shouts, 'Say hi to the guys.' I tell Walter that somebody should shoot Julio before he kills someone. Walter doesn't say anything. Two weeks later Julio gets killed when he tries to rob a drunkard who happened to be an off-duty cop. The news makes me happy.

Undated

The train is still packed and once again not moving an inch. People stare at their shiny little screens; their necks will hurt later on. A montage of long miserable faces and then cut to green fields, beaches, Paris, prairies, Kathmandu, Shangri-La, Siberia, Tokyo, Iceland, Cape Verde, lakes and mountains, or just Blackpool — anywhere the passengers would rather be. And a wide river. And Prague. And Dublin.

2:34 a.m., August 17, 2006

Marcos is talking and talking and talking and I listen and drink and listen and drink. We're in a place called Clair de Lune in Montmartre, the only place we could find open. Sabina is here. She doesn't drink and frowns every time I take the wine glass to my mouth. Marcos speaks in Argentinian and I listen in Argentinian and someone else is speaking in Argentinian at the back of the bar. Someone insults someone else in Argentinian at the back of the bar. There's some pushing and shoving and someone leaves and the space between us and the back of the bar is cleared and I see Walter. We stare at each other and move fast between the tables and chairs and we embrace. We can't believe we're both here, in Paris of all places, living the cliché of the Argentine 'intellectual' abroad. We stare at each other as if we are hallucinating and maybe we are. But it's great to see we've both got out of Rosario and didn't end up in Miami, speaking in Cuban. He comes up to our table and now does the talking and we get seriously drunk, Marcos, Walter and I.

8:57 a.m., December 12, 2014

And to make matters worse he's just received an email from a literary mag saying the editors have read a fiction piece he submitted almost a year ago: the editors have read your piece with interest, and although they found it well written the editors do not appreciate the jolts in time; they also felt that the ending was inconclusive, as if this story was a fragment from a broader story. They now want him to edit it considering their comments. The problem is the piece is called 'Jolts' and is precisely about jolts in time and space, about how some of us are more sensitive to fragments and how some of us are more fragmented than the rest, particularly on some days.

11:34 p.m., September 10, 2008

I can feel my stomach coming through my mouth as I kneel before the toilet seat. Nothing comes out of my mouth besides my stomach because there's nothing else in there — I'm vomiting fear. Sabina is standing by the door, saying she's sorry but that she's got to do it. She's holding a small Samsonite suitcase, my suitcase. And she does it, she leaves and takes off for Prague the following morning. And I don't see her for over a year, until we meet to sign the divorce papers and she gives me back my suitcase. It's my favourite suitcase.

9:23 a.m., December 12, 2014

The editors do not appreciate your jolts in time. Everything about that statement makes him sick: the academic snobbery of avoiding contractions, the passive aggressive 'appreciate' instead of a right-out 'hate', their use of the third person plural. Who are the editors? Why don't they appreciate his jolts in time? How do they live lives without jolts? What do they mean by 'inconclusive'? Should the piece end with a description of Armageddon? How can anything be conclusive when there's always the next fragment to come? He wishes them death. He wishes them that conclusiveness. Before they kill someone.

10:43 p.m., February 16, 1998

The square is called Plaza de los Locos — there used to be an asylum here twenty years or so ago. Cristian, Julio, Chor, and Esteban are here with me; we're drinking warm white wine and smoking and we're pretty drunk and stoned. Julio fidgets for a while in his pocket and gets a small replica gun out. He points it at Cristian and pulls the trigger and the hammer makes a dry noise. We all laugh. Then he points it at me but doesn't pull the trigger. He points it at Chor and pulls the trigger and there's that dry sound and we all laugh again. Then the same with Esteban. 'This is the one I used to rob those wankers,' he says and points it to the ground and pulls the trigger and there's this loud BANG! and a bullet bounces on the floor leaving a tiny cloud before it disappears into the night. Julio's face briskly turns pale and Chor jumps up, pulls the gun from Julio's hand and slaps him across the face. Julio falls from the bench and Chor moves to him, mounts him, and starts slapping him with the front and the back of his hand, calling him a 'snotty cunt' over and over again until we stop him. Now Julio's nose is bleeding and his right eye starts to swell. We leave him there crying and go to the pier to throw the gun into the river.

We throw it as far as we can, hoping it will sink into the canal that used to carry the big transatlantic cargos before the ships stopped coming and everyone started to talk about leaving.

Undated

An empty carriage by the platform. Litter, free newspapers, paper cups, a forgotten smartphone. The doors are open. There's nobody in the station save for a couple of guards. It starts snowing once again. A beautiful snow that gets into the train and slowly melts into a shapeless mud.

9:43 a.m., December 12, 2014

The editors never appreciate anything and if they do they just sit on it, like with his second book, that only sold forty-three copies and that the publisher refused to promote any further after the launch party because people in Spain and Latin America don't really read books anymore, you should write something in English for us, they told him. And he did — for someone else — and even swore never to write in Spanish again. But he knows very well books won't get him where he needs to be or anywhere at all and he's been waiting for the trains to move in this station café for two hours. He should just break camp and go home. When you spend time in terminals you're always at the mercy of terrorists. He should just head home, hide his head under his pillow. It's impossible to keep on living like this, at the mercy of terrorists, editors and trains.

9:13 p.m., January 16, 2009

'That was the same question!' 'No! Not at all!' 'Yes, it was! YOU WANKER!' says Marcos, 'I told you not to fuck around with the i-Ching. I TOLD YOU!' 'I asked a different question, I swear!' 'It's giving you the same answer: the same hexagram and the same changes. That's because you asked the same question. I told you not to ask the same question. You shouldn't play with this!'

It's nighttime and soon we'll be heading to a gig down République's way. I'm living in Paris once more, once more a suitcase and a short-term teaching job at Paris VIII. It's true I asked the same question and I probably broke the i-Ching and things will never make sense again, because the question was exactly 'Will things ever make sense again?' 'I'll never do this again for you. Never again,' he says. 'I'm sorry,' I say. 'You have some thinking to do, bro.' 'What did I get, again?' '虎,' he says.

10:23 p.m., December 19, 2001

It's impossibly hot and people are wild tonight, even with the curfew. Guille and Manuel are watching the protests in Buenos Aires with Ludmila; I'm rolling under the table with Milena, Ludmila's sister, while I fondle Ludmila's leg. Ludmila pushes my hand away several times until she stops pushing and spreads her legs. Milena finds it funny and she pulls Ludmila towards us but Ludmila stays on the table with the other two, mesmerised by the screen. Suddenly the cops start killing people, the president takes off for Uruguay in a helicopter, and four more presidents fail to secure a government in the space of two weeks. In a couple of months I'm on a flight to Dublin, without the faintest idea of what I'll do with the rest of my life. I'll start washing dishes the morning after arriving and then spend the next thirteen years changing rooms in several cities. But I'm not thinking this right there with Milena — there and then I'm young, careless, stupid, libertine, and probably free.

9:47 a.m., December 12, 2014

An empty table. Croissant crumbs. A half-full café latte in a cardboard cup. A seat, still warm.

9:43 a.m., July 3, 1986

We're fishing with my grandad. We've jumped a wall to get into this abandoned stretch of beach, where the sand plant used to be. I pierce the hook through a worm and it wiggles. It makes me feel a bit sick but it's still a happy moment, only us three, me and my grandad and the worm.

Undated

The empty train as seen from the station. Then, black. If writing had sound it would be possible to hear the empty train station and London in the background, over the black page.

ONLY UP HERE

Midday. I've been rolling around in bed since I quit last week. It happened out of nowhere: I pulled myself a double Jameson's during a busy shift and sat on the other side of the bar. What are you doing? I'm quitting. You can't quit. Yes I can: look. Go have a fag and come back behind the bar. I won't — it's too busy behind the bar. You've got to give me at least a week's notice. Silence. I finished my drink and walked out of the pub with the voice of the Cypriot telling me I was barred. I left with most of my money in my pocket; not that they would ever notice — they could never get the till right. And then I felt like I owned the world, that I could go anywhere. London was finally smiling at me: no more bar jobs, no more mopping the floor, collecting pints, long shifts serving entitled drunk wankers. The beginning of a new era; a new me; then it was already the future and the future of that future was full of promises. The high lasted for a couple of hours. Soon I realised I was unemployed. And I hit the bed. I must have been in bed for five days.

Not exactly five days in bed but five days of leaving it only to go for a piss, grab something to eat, smoke a cigarette by the window, have a drink of water. And the same happened to Leo: he fell into introspection at about the same time — two days before me, actually. My moments of ecstasy and sadness were probably a copycat version of his, after he quit his job at the Bricklayer's Arms. He had come home hyperventilated, coked-up, speaking about his plans to go back to film school and do a film version of Fogwill's *Los pichiciegos*, how we should rent a car on Sunday and drive to Cambridge, Oxford, Kent, Cornwall, whatever, like Thelma and Louise, he said and laughed. And then the bed. Just like I would some days later.

And now midday all through this side of the studio flat and on Leo's side too. I'm head-to-the-pillow when the sun comes through the huge window. The smell of feet in the room, burnt cigarette butts, lack of personal and general hygiene, the mess all around us, a space too small for two guys. And we ran out of cunting cigarettes too, says Leo. Go get some, I say. Fuck off, he says, not even raising his head from the pillow. Anyway, it's only a matter of holding on until tonight. Maybe I'll even fall asleep and wake up tomorrow. I wish I could sleep until the next year.

By two p.m. I can't take it anymore and leave the flat. It's stupidly sunny while I make my way to George's Kebab, just around the corner. I walk into his shop with my stomach rumbling and don't even say hi until I've ordered my food: a large shish with humus and a can of ginger beer. Hello first, innit? Hello George! Sorry, I'm really hungry. No worries my friend we'll feed you. Nice to see you; where were you?

he asks. I was away, at a training course to join the Royal Marines, I say. I thought you had to be British to join the army, he says. They've relaxed the rules now; they need people from other backgrounds. How did the training go? I passed it! Good on you, son. But I've changed my mind, I don't think the army is for me. Yes, don't join these English cunts on anything. I won't! Cunts all of them. Large shish and humus and a can of ginger beer; there you go my friend, he says, and nods towards the back.

Soon I'm sitting in the back room, accidentally watching Newell's Old Boys, my team from Argentina, playing a shitty football game; the commentary is in Turkish — it's all very strange. Eleven thousand one hundred and forty-six kilometres away, I'm watching twenty-two idiots chase a ball in real time. With three or four seconds delay, perhaps, but live. It's mind-boggling. From Rosario and across the Atlantic, over the Ural mountains, BANG!, Istanbul, then picked up by a Soviet satellite who-knows-how-many kilometres above the atmosphere and BANG! (again) on the telly before me. I tell an old leather-jacket-clad Turk about this uncanny situation. I think he doesn't understand me — he just smiles blankly and then goes back to his paper. I shut up and eat my kebab.

The other guy is here as well — the guy with the weird little eye, the second-in-command. He calls me 'my friend' too. He soon spots me and sits on the table with me. He asks where I have been and I tell him I've been working overtime, managing the pub isn't an easy job, you see. Then I tell him they fired me. He seems confused, puzzled, or perhaps just drunk. He says something about these fucking English cunts being lazy backstabbers. I tell him the owners of the place are Cypriots. He says they must be Greek Cypriots. I say I'm pretty sure they're Turkish Cypriots. He doesn't reply and stops talking to me for a while. Then he says that there are cunts everywhere — he's absolutely right. He's drinking raki and his eye, the funky one, gets smaller with every sip. By the end of the bottle he'll look like Thom Yorke. But before that happens my team scores a goal and I celebrate by closing my fist and saying yessssss. Little Eye celebrates too — he hugs me and gets a bit overexcited and drops his glass on the floor — it shatters to pieces. He curses in Turkish and leaves the room. The accident doesn't seem to bother the rest of the guys in here — they're all busy staring at a laptop, hypnotised by it. Kebab people love gadgets — they are technological people.

Little Eye comes back and sweeps the floor with a broom, stumbling and singing something in Turkish.

This incredible universe of brands, smells, little and medium-sized tins and cans, unpronounceable names and inedible processed meals.

The off-licence guy asks me where I've been. I tell him I was on a meditation retreat on the Isle of Man. I don't even know how I come up with this. He doesn't say anything for a while. Then he asks me about my job, did I take a holiday? I say I've quit and he frowns. I pay for the beers, the Supermalt and the Jaffa cakes. Thanks. You're welcome. A frown, a clearly annoyed frown. He says that I have to work now that I'm young so that I can retire well when I'm older. I knew he would come up with some shit like that. I tell him that I've got a job interview in the City this week, for Royal Bank of Scotland, and that's why I quit my job at the bar and went on a meditation retreat. He says I should have quit only after being sure I got the job. I say I needed time to prepare for the job interview — god, I hate hard-working people. He asks me what sort of meditation I practise. I ask what does he mean with what kind? Vipassana, Zen, Mindfulness? he asks. It's all the same, I say. No, it isn't. He seems to know all about it. I say Singing Yoga Meditation. Singing Yoga Meditation? He seems confused. I tell him we do yoga, sing and then meditate. I don't think he buys it. It's a sort of New Age thing, very popular round Dalston. Never heard of it. It's a new thing. Then he asks me about 'my friend Leo' managing to sound the quotation marks. I tell him that he's still at the retreat, that he decided to stay a bit longer, he's getting good at the singing yoga but needs to improve on the meditative side of things. He quit his job too? Yes, he did. He has an interview at Warner Brothers the same day I have mine at Royal Bank of Scotland. You two are doing fine, he says. It was about time, I say. He tells me to remind Leo that he owes him twenty pounds. I say I will. When's your interview, he asks. On Wednesday, I say. Good luck to you both. I thank him and walk out.

It's three p.m. and still very sunny. I cross the road and walk towards St Leonard's churchyard. When I'm halfway there I feel I need to go for a piss. So I backtrack and head to the public toilets on the corner of Columbia and Hackney roads, some hundred metres up. There aren't many people around save for some hipsters carrying flowers and plants from the flower market. Perhaps I should go and buy a plant or just walk to the market, see people, maybe bump into someone I know, have a coffee, get some clean air.

A couple of minutes pass and the door remains locked. I look at a couple passing by, a girl and a guy; the girl with skinny legs, flat ass and huge tits, the guy very tall and pale, quite good looking, but he's wearing flip-flops and has huge bony feet. They stare at me when they pass — it must be my plastic bag. And then they're gone. Some more people carrying plants, the phone booth; I start to get bored. I remember when I called Guido from this phone booth soon after I arrived. I called him crying, paying for the phone call with pound coins, saying that I was freaking out because I was feeling suicidal and was missing Rosario, if that is even possible — it was a very expensive phone call. Why do you say that? I don't really know; it's just this horrible idea I can't get out of my head: I think I'll kill myself. Have you been using drugs? No. Since when do you have this in your head? Since I arrived, I said, London is a shithole. I don't know why I called him, of all the people back home. I guess I needed to speak to someone and his was the only number I remembered at the time. Suddenly I ran out of coins and the call ended. It must have been a disturbing phone call, because he started emailing me like mad afterward, saying that I was very selfish calling him out of the blue like that, that he had to ask around to find out if I was still alive, that I should have at least called him back to tell him I hadn't killed myself. I never replied to his emails but he kept sending them. I thought he would just let it go but he didn't give up. So I blocked him. He changed his email and I blocked him again and he changed the email address and so on: the whole process went on for a while. Until I tired and changed my email and gave it only to my mother and father. But he got hold of my phone number and started calling me until I changed my number too. I should never have called him that day: he's fucking insane.

The door finally opens and one of the local crackheads leaves. He bows in a friendly way and I say hi. He's high and looks very happy. The door closes behind him and there's a sound of water; the word 'cleaning' starts flashing in red on the door and we both stare at it and it's fascinating. Until he gets bored and walks away. When he's walked some twenty metres he turns around and waves with a broad smile. I wave back at him, just about the same time the word 'cleaning' stops flashing. I put 20p in the slot and the door opens and I walk in. It looks pretty clean: no sign of drug paraphernalia, no weird smells, no small pieces of cotton. Perhaps he was really in need of a toilet.

I struggle for a bit first but then manage to piss with my plastic bag in one hand. A nice piss, longer than expected, but a bit dark, perhaps from having my kidneys crushed during my last few days in bed. It feels great to piss in a different toilet — I can see things are beginning to move. When I finish I leave without washing my hands because my dick must be cleaner than the faucet. The door opens and I leave. The door closes behind me and the flushing sound starts once more.

Sunny, so sunny. The traffic as a background mantra and traces of fumes in the air. I'm sitting on a bench in the middle of the churchyard, checking out the tombstones in the distance and drinking my Supermalt. There are a couple of crackheads — others — loitering about. A guy, around thirty, and a girl, who could be anything from seventeen to fifty-five. They've been around the yard, picking up cigarette butts and putting them in their pockets and scavenging who knows what from the trash bins.

Now they're arguing by the church entrance. I can't hear what they say, but she shouts louder than him. She moves her hands like a Neapolitan; a lot of hands being thrown into the air in all directions — crack makes people very expressive. Or she must be communicating something very important, or maybe she just talks like that, like a Neapolitan; or maybe she is a Neapolitan. I've seen this couple before many times since I moved to Waterson Street. They hang around with the public toilet crackhead, mostly around the churchyard, although I've seen them walking up and down Old Street, begging for money and tobacco from the wankers late on Fridays and Saturdays. Crackheads are always in fast forward, always in a rush to get somewhere. Many times I've thought I should stop one of them and ask what's the rush?

It's getting hot and humid now; it's getting dark; it'll rain. I light up one of my counterfeit Polish Marlboro. Smoking feels funny: smoke gets denser and the cigarettes smokier. The fag doesn't taste right, and it smells weird, and I can't tell whether it's the humidity or this is the taste of Eastern Europe.

Back in the off-licence I buy a new lighter, a can of tuna, mozzarella, baked beans and crisps. I ask the guy to swap my cans for cold ones. He agrees but he checks that the cans haven't been opened. I know he thinks I'm a lazy fuck and that he doesn't trust me; I don't trust him either. He's always checking the CCTV screen when I walk to the back of the shop and I'm always checking the expiry date on the products. He tells me once more to remind Leo about his twenty pounds. I say I will, and think to myself that he's bound to live out his days behind the counter of his tiny shop, until he gets his throat cut from ear to ear by one of the churchyard bums.

Things are better next door. No need for CCTV when you have a large kebab knife behind the counter. I buy three more packs of cigarettes from Little Eye. Palenia Zabija. Palenia Zabija, I say, reading the writing on the pack, chcesz papierosa. Eight pounds my friend, he says. Three for eight pounds. Even if they taste like shit: long live the EU, long live Poland and continental pulmonary conditions.

Soon I get home. I open the door. Leo is still tucked under the sheets. He looks at me when I enter the flat. Hi, I say, I got us food. Morning, he says. It's four thirty, I answer. He doesn't reply and I'm starting to get tired of his self-pity. I'll cook some food, I say. More silence.

I walk towards the kitchen area and open a drawer and get the tin opener. I open the can of tuna and empty it into a medium-sized bowl. I open the baked beans and mix the beans with the tuna. I put the mix in the microwave oven, set it for three minutes. While the tuna and the beans are turning I put the beers in the fridge. Then I get the mozzarella out of the pack and lay it on a plate. I watch the bowl turn in the oven and soon the thing beeps a couple of times. I cut the mozzarella in two and then open the oven and get the bowl out and empty some of the tuna and beans from the bowl into the plate; then I put one of the halves of mozzarella in the bowl. There you go, you need to eat something, I say, holding a plate to Leo's face. I'm not hungry, he says. Eat anyway; I've got cigarettes, a lot of them; but no ciggies until you've eaten. Which ones? George's or the cabbies'? George's. Lights or reds? Lights. I like reds, he says. I don't, I say. I leave the plate next to Leo's bed and go to my side of the room. I'm hungry and I eat fast. Before I finish my plate I see Leo grabbing his. He starts eating, slowly.

It'll rain, I say. Yes, he answers. It's very muggy out there. Yes, it feels muggy in here too. I got us some beers; I thought we could go to the roof, drink beer, smoke, listen to music. It'll rain, he says. We can hide under the water tank. I'm not sure I want to go all the way up, he says, sorry. No worries, I say, I'll go by myself.

I finish eating from my bowl and leave it by the side of the bed. I move my clothes around until I find my small CD player. I press play to see if the batteries are still good—it would seem so, at least the CD seems to be moving: THESUNDAYSTHESUNDAYS. The letters become one large white lump and I press stop. I can feel Leo staring at me but I don't look back. I get my cigarettes and keys, grab the beers from the fridge and leave. I'll be on the roof, I say before I close the door.

The parking lot and the flats all around. Three blocks in a

square of which the fourth side leads to an alley, some more workshops, or the end of the world for all I know. And here four floors of huge windows, converted workshops, tall ceilings and cold lofty spaces — places never meant to be lived in, and yet here we are. There are traces of fabrics being scattered by the wind and some weird cylindrical props rolling on the floor. A huge cardboard palm tree lays next to the overfilled garbage skip. A flash flares in one of the few flats with curtains. Someone shouts in Italian in one of the flats below me. A girl laughs somewhere. Five cool-looking people are barbecuing something on the roof to my right. People are going about their lives in their flats and the sky is bright yellow. I haven't opened a can yet, I haven't lit up yet, I haven't even pressed play. I'm just sitting here, under the water tank, looking around, not thinking much.

Thunder, finally, and Leo's hand resting on my shoulder. He sits by my side, wrapped inside one of his sheets — a stinking greasy-haired Jesus Christ. I pass him the Polish Marlboros and he lights up. I'm glad you came, I say. It's windy, he says.

Beers are opened — no need for a toast.

We drink in silence and smoke.

We both look at the sky.

It can't be long before the clouds fall down like sacks of potatoes. But the barbecue people on the other roof don't seem to care. Perhaps they haven't even realised or perhaps they've reached an ideal state of unawareness of the things around them. Shit, Leo says, it will rain like in the Bible. Yes, I say. I've left the windows open, he says. Don't worry Leo, we're only up here. He nods and I press play.

TURKISH DELIGHT

At vos quo lubet hinc abite, lymphae, vini
pernicies, et ad severos migrate.
CATULLUS

'Can I get you a drink?' Nick asked as soon as I crossed the door. I said yes and three minutes into my visit I was sipping a Long Island Ice Tea while listening to Astor Piazzolla, who Nick had perhaps chosen to make me feel welcome.

His place was this huge conversion overlooking Leinster Square, second floor, a lovely flat. He was working on the food in the kitchen, occasionally shouting some of his impressions about the music. Nothing of what he said was really interesting or avoided the commonplace, but he had cooked a Sunday roast, with Yorkshire pudding and all the trimmings. This was the first time an Englishman had invited me to his house since moving to London. And this is something that, as I would discover since then, doesn't happen that often.

'This is sublime,' he said, referring to the music, one of the times he showed up in the lounge to top up my glass with Diet Coke.

'Yes, it's fine,' I said.

'No, it's not "just fine" — it's sublime,' he said.

'Yes, it's sublime,' I said and he seemed pleased with my reply and went back into the kitchen.

Nick always had Turkish Delight at hand. Second-or third-rate London Turkish Delight, but Turkish Delight nevertheless. And he looked as if he had already done some. He seemed overexcited. Or maybe it was just my imagination, my own craving. In any case I thought it wouldn't have been appropriate to force a conversation about this topic, not so soon and with him being so generous as to have me over, so I decided to give him until after lunch. Then I would get my own out and invite him. I was, of course, hoping he would feel pity and let me have his instead, because I didn't have much left at all.

Nick had nice furniture but the flat looked cold. It could have passed for one of those showrooms they have in new buildings. Everything was too perfect, too anal, too clean, shiny, uninhabited. And the screen on his TV set was covered with text. Nick had once mentioned that he used to spend his weekends watching football teletext but I hadn't taken him seriously. Yet here it was, this constant parade of letters on the screen, never-ending. No volume, no image, just letters. No doubt he could have afforded cable but I guess it had to do with his work as a stockbroker and a fetish for data displayed on screens, not that I cared much about telly at that moment. I was just sitting there, observing, mentally calculating how much the rent for this kind of pad would cost, whether he owned. I was inclined towards the latter: he looked like the kind of person who owns; he looked like the kind of person who buys at the right moment, sells at the right moment, and retires somewhere sunny to live off his savings and spends all his remaining days and most of his pension doing Turkish Delight.

'The food is ready!' shouted Nick from the kitchen and I walked over there. A nice kitchen too, as shiny and clean as the lounge. There were two or three cooking books on a table and a centrepiece with fake fruits. We ate sitting at a bar. The food was OK; the wine was better.

And soon we were snorting my Turkish Delight from a metallic tray with an advert for Bacardi in the middle, using a rolled-up five-pound note. The stuff was enough for two shots each and I made it clear that I didn't have any more left.

'We should go and buy some more,' he said. 'Turkish Delight goes really well with Sunday afternoons. We should go, get some more, and then hit the road, have something to drink down Portobello Road, hit the record shops, stop here and there to top up every half an hour or so, and then come back home, listen to some new records and maybe call a couple of whores in to finish the weekend with full colours!' — apparently, Turkish Delight made him talkative.

'OK,' I replied — Turkish Delight always makes me quiet.

'Yes. These are good plans. I like them, yes. Very good plans. I think this is the way to go today, tonight. Get properly turked up, get laid, have a nice party. You know the deal!'

'Sure. But I'm skint Nick. I've got only twenty pounds left until I get paid next week.'

'No worries. I'll sort you out and sort the Turkish Delight and the girls out. No worries, mate. Money is not an issue, mate. You would do the same for me, wouldn't you? If you weren't a poor and stingy piece of shit, ha, ha!'

'Sure. I'd do the same if I could. Where can we get Turkish Delight, then?'

'I was hoping that was something you could sort out…'

'My pusher lives in East London.'

'I see… Not to worry… Not to worry. We'll sort something out. Notting Hill is Turkeyland on Sundays.'

'Cool.'

'Have another Long Island Ice Tea, mate. Ha ha! We'll have a smashing afternoon. Ha ha! I love good plans. I love it, mate. Love it! Fucking great. A plus. You are a good lad!'

He started to fix two more drinks while I went to the toilet. Every time Turkish Delight is discussed and/or snorted I need to go empty my bowels. I don't know why but that's the way it is.

The toilet was a nice, clean one. I didn't have to juggle shitting standing up. There was a magazine rack by the toilet seat and I picked up a copy of *Men's Health*. Seeing all these beefed-up guys with six packs and veiny necks helped me finish quite fast. And soon, after cleaning myself with good quality toilet paper, I was washing my hands and face with a delicious lavender soap, from L'Occitane. It was a nice day. Yes, it was turning out fine.

The Turkish Delight started to wear off at the exact moment we were passing by a kitchenware shop in Londsdale Road, where everything seemed unbearably shiny and expensive. I figured out the impending crisis when I tried to speak to Nick and felt my tongue tied. I think he felt it too because he made a passing remark about how soon we would reach that pub in Portobello Road and look for Dennis Ahmed, this estate agent he knew, who would surely sort out some Turkish Delight for us. It was sunny but there were dark clouds lingering up above. It was clear it was going to rain. It was just a matter of time — it's always a matter of time.

Portobello Road was packed with tourists checking out stalls; they were all dressed in beige and wearing gigantic white trainers and had massive cameras — it was harrowing. We walked on the sidewalk, as far as we could from the crowd, almost crushing ourselves against the walls, and we walked fast, as fast as we could.

And soon we reached the pub. It was packed as well. We walked in and went straight to the bar. Nick gave me a tenner and asked me to buy a couple of beers. He said he was going to look for Dennis Ahmed in the back room. I elbowed my way to the front of the bar and stayed there, holding the ten-pound note with my arm outstretched. I didn't make any attempt to make eye contact with the barman but somehow I ended up ordering two pints of Red Stripe. And after paying I made my way out of the crowd and outside. I rested the drinks on the windowpane and lit a cigarette. A couple of minutes later Nick showed up, with a grave expression on his face.

'Can't find Dennis Ahmed,' he said.

'Call him.'

'I don't have his number. I don't think he works like that.'

'Have a drink then,' I said and he drank half his pint in one go before I had finished speaking.

'Maybe we can find him down the road, in the Duke of Wellington,' he said.

'Let's try,' I said.

So we downed the rest of our beers and went to this other pub just a minute away. And there we found Dennis Ahmed, sitting on the terrace. Dennis Ahmed was this relatively big guy with a Middle Eastern face. He was with two girls, one white and the other black, both very pretty, wearing pumps and jeans and Wayfarers, and very likely high on Turkish Delight. Dennis Ahmed grinned when he saw Nick.

'Give me a couple of minutes. Grab a table inside and get some drinks,' Nick said, handing me a twenty-pound note this time.

'OK,' I said and went in.

I was already quite drunk but still operational. I went to the bar and bought two pints of Red Stripe and two shots of tequila, pocketed the change, and grabbed a table by the toilet. I waited for a couple of minutes and when Nick didn't show up I downed one shot and then the other. Nick crossed the door a few seconds later, this time smiling.

'That's it. We've got some to get along,' he said, standing up by the table, and then grabbed his pint and had a sip. 'He'll sort three grams out for later.'

'Cool.'

'I'll be back,' Nick said and went into the toilet. He came back after two or three minutes and pushed his cigarettes across the table. I got the cigarettes and went to the toilet myself. There was music playing in there, different music than in the pub. The Smiths; a song I liked. I went into the cubicle and did two shots of Turkish Delight with my Argentine driving license. After I licked the license I realised it had expired. I went out, sat at the table and handed the cigarettes back to Nick. Soon I was feeling OK again. Turkish Delight is great; A-plus, I thought.

We were supposed to come back in a couple of hours to pick up the rest of the score, so we finished our drinks and left. Dennis Ahmed was no longer sitting on the terrace but the two girls were still there. Nick went to their table and said something I couldn't get from a distance — they laughed. And then we headed towards the record shops near Notting Hill Gate. Both of us were walking fast and I was in a good mood. Nick was doing the talking, again.

'They've got a good jazz selection over there. Very cheap. You can find almost everything worth finding there. Sometimes the vinyls are a bit scratched. So be careful: have a proper look before buying. I've got Billie Holiday singing the first line of "You've Changed" on repeat, you know, like when you get a song stuck in your head... Have a proper look, I know what I'm telling you. You've changed. You've changed. You've changed. Does my head in.'

'OK.'

It was very sunny, so sunny that it was impossible to see the faces of the people walking the other way. The sun hitting my eyes and not being able to see faces felt good. The clouds had disappeared.

'And it's a lot better than Rough Trade,' Nick went on. 'You can only get overpriced indie stuff in Rough Trade and the staff are a bunch of cunts. They've been screwed up by *High Fidelity*. Fuck Nick Hornby and fuck John Cusack, and that shit film, man. They ruined the record shop industry. Have you been to Rough Trade lately? It's unbearable.'

'What's a Rough Trade?'

'Don't you know?'

'No.'

'It's a record shop!'

'Never been there.'

'Gosh! You need to get out more, mate. You spend too much time indoors writing shit.'

'True.'

'Anyway. What are you after? Let me guess: the Beatles. All you guys like the Beatles. You surely must want a Beatles LP, to keep as a souvenir, to hang it on the wall, *Sergeant Pepper*, or some crap like that.'

'No.'

'You must be after some prog rock then. You look like a prog rock fan.'

'I don't like prog rock.'

'Really?'

'I actually hate it.'

'You do well, mate! Goblin-loving wankers wearing their fucking golden capes. I'd shoot the whole lot of them. All fucking nerds.'

We reached the end of Portobello Road and took a right turn.

'I'm after something by The Smiths.'

'Really? Who would have thought... Well, they used to be good. Even if Morrissey was always a bit of a knobhead, right? What album?'

'Not sure. Do you know that song about the guy who's looking for a job and finds it and then feels pretty bad?'

'Strikes a bell.'

'Just heard it in the toilet. I want that song.'

'Cool. Ask the attendant. Anyway, let's stop here for a pint and a top up,' he said pointing towards the Sun in Splendour.

'So soon?'

'Yes! We can't be topping up in a record shop, can we?'

'Right.'

This time I went to the toilet first while he went to the bar to get the drinks. I did two shots, once for each nostril, and licked the license. The Turkish Delight was going down quickly and after Nick's turn we would have just enough for a couple of shots each. We would have to time things wisely, if we didn't want to end up turkless before meeting Dennis Ahmed. I went out.

'There's only half left. We'll have to time this right,' I said and passed the cigarettes to Nick.

'Don't worry. It's just over two hours till Dennis' time. Have a drink,' he said and left for the toilet.

I drank from my beer and looked around. The pub was full of beautiful people. Blond guys in red jeans and white shirts, sweaters wrapped around their necks, loafers no socks; blonde girls in summer dresses and Wayfarers (indoors), wearing pumps, sandals, some wearing Chuck Taylors, one or two barefoot, pretty feet. If it hadn't been for the Turkish Delight, that held everything around me together like a coherent living organism of which I was a part, I would have felt sad and out of place. But I felt I belonged, in some way, like an epiphanic cancer from a story in *Reader's Digest*. There was a place for me there, yes there was, however anomalous. And I dreaded the thought of losing all this, having it taken away from me too soon, just because we couldn't find Dennis Ahmed again.

Nick came out of the toilet, smiling, happy — I guess he belonged too; I guess he always already belonged without so many thoughts. He came to my side and leaned against the bar.

'Cheers buddy!' he said and we toasted.

Nick looked around the pub for a few moments and then at his phone.

'Where are we meeting this guy?' I asked.

'You mean Dennis Ahmed?'

'Yeah…'

'Worried?'

'A bit, yes.'

'Don't be, mate, don't be.'

'Did you give him money?'

'Yes. But don't worry. He'll turn up, he always turns up, he's reliable, as reliable as an estate agent can be. Cheer up buddy!' he grabbed my elbow and shook me a bit; I was pretty stiff. And yes, I was starting to get seriously worried. But I didn't let the worry take over — I couldn't spoil this almost perfect moment.

'I'm cool,' I said. 'I'm cool, Nick!'

'We are having a ball, buddy! Chin-chin!' And we toasted again.

'Gotta go to the loo,' I said and Nick nodded.

It was a sweaty affair because I had to do some acrobatics on the dirty toilet seat. But it was fast and soon I was out again.

Nick was chatting with the barmaid.

'Right, mate?' he said.

'Right,' I said. The girl smiled and I smiled back. She was blonde, of course, but dyed blonde.

'Shall we go and get those records?'

'Sure,' I said.

'Thanks,' he said to the barmaid and we left.

METHYLATED SPIRITS

Nous souffrons par les rêves. Nous guérissons par les rêves.
GASTON BACHELARD

We apologise for the long waiting times at the tills as I'm pushing or pulling my zebra-patterned trolley. Pushing or pulling with my left hand, my right hand with its fingers wrapped around the handle of a shopping basket. There must be thousands of us, moving chaotically and at different speeds, a whim of hungry and thirsty people who left everything until too late. And the sound of the wheels and the music playing in the background: dizzying, a weird muzak-like mantra sprinkled with dissonant overtones, barely audible over the noise, yet there. And the voices, muffled. And the mobile phones ringing unattended. And the faint infant shrieks and the unrecognisable growls, of joy or despair. And the other voices barking through the tannoy, accented and contrite and we apologise for the long waiting times at the tills, Sainsbury's would like to assure you that everything is being done to guarantee that you have a great shopping experience; Merry Christmas! Someone, actual people and not a recording, over and over, every other couple of minutes, word by word. It could be unnerving, yet an endearing hint of humanity can be discerned in these messages, in their tiny imperfections, in the repressed alienation and boredom of those sending these repetitive bottled messages into the void, for the minimum wage, at four-thirty p.m., on 24 December.

Now by the vegetables section, by the cabbage, unable to move in any direction. An old lady with furious blue hair a couple of metres down is blocking the way — she's surrounded by trolleys — she seems trapped. It looks bad but we're all taking it rather well: no arguing, no pushing or shoving, no scenes of panic or collapse of the social order. Nothing save the occasional tut — there must be tut-tuts going on; timid tut-tuts and huffs masked by the ambient noise. We tut and huff unheard and wait for the old lady to figure out how to manoeuvre out of this mess. We wait, resigned. Keep calm and carry on, waiting.

Several minutes elapse and my phone battery goes from 91 to 73 while I read an opinion piece about a gadget that can detect your body odour and tell you if you need a deodorant — very useful if you happen to lose the sense of smell, according to the barely literate writer. So to stop the battery from reaching zero, and to keep what little intelligence I have left after reading the article, I check my list, a crumpled blue A4 sheet of paper: asparagus, shallots, parsley, coriander, new potatoes and some other stuff. And suddenly the old lady summons the courage, leaves the trolley unattended for a couple of seconds, grabs a bag of broccoli, comes back to her spot, and continues to move forward, pushing the other trolleys to the sides with hers.

We are free, the knot unknotted, we're moving.

And soon some meat products, we apologise for the long waiting times, we would like to assure you that everything is being done so that you have a great shopping experience. Turkey fillets, minced beef, on my mind. But I'm going too fast and I slow down a bit and I feel a bump: a guy following me close has hit me with his own Sainsbury's trolley. He doesn't apologise and I don't say anything. I just redistribute my weight and my trolley gets heavier and he can't push anymore, while I dawdle to the left, feeling the weight of all his shopping, and then cut across to the other side, almost barging into a large woman with two large boys, seven to eight. I block their way with my basket, placing it at the height of the children's faces. The two identically bloated gammon faces stop and then my body follows and after my body the trolley.

I grab two packs of turkey fillets and suddenly a hunch hits me as we apologise for the overcrowding and the long waiting times, once again, Merry Christmas! The list: asparagus, shallots, parsley, coriander, new potatoes, turkey fillets, mince beef, cream, cheddar, butter. Down: toilet paper. Further down: mustard. Even further down: methylated spirits or firestarter fuel. A question mark next to these; I turn the page over. Chicken fillets, I knew it.

The chicken fillets are lying a bare metre down. I get two packs. British chicken, Union Jacked.

I make it to the end of the aisle and take a right turn. Trolleys here move with the order that arises out of chaos, given chaos enough time and space.

And then a left turn.

This aisle promises a world of dairy and cold meats and then cheese on my side and microwaveable foods on the other. Not many people round here — cheese people are now a diminishing demographic, suspiciously continental. I get a pack of cheddar — there is nothing but cheddar. Cheddar will have to do. I get three extra packs, in different shades of orange.

Now there are three lanes: two slow lanes by the fridges, where people move with difficulty, their direction and movements decided by the products; and one in the middle, a fast lane. On the sides, people wait with their trolleys in the ready position and then throw themselves seagull-like into the first available gap and disappear towards the fruits section, we apologise for the waiting times at the tills. I find a gap and disappear too.

More stasis, by the red grapes and the bananas. I rest the basket on my trolley and gauge the curvature of the bananas and don't know what to think, my mind consumed with trying to imagine ways of getting out of this jam. I'm trapped between an abandoned fully loaded Sainsbury's trolley and two old ladies chatting behind me. I have tried several times to push one of the abandoned trolleys without success, as the wheels are locked and end up banging against the aisle — I can't move it from this angle. And it would be impolite to interrupt the old ladies' conversation to make a move towards the other end — they seemed to be talking about religious fundamentalists, although now they seem to be talking about the weather.

I look at my phone — 65 per cent left — and then at my list: all pretty straightforward until mustard. Which mustard? Dijon? English? American? Methylated spirits or firestarter fuel? Do they still stock Dijon in this supermarket, we apologise for the long waiting times at the tills, we would like to assure you that everything is being done to guarantee that you have a great shopping experience, Merry Christmas? And where are you supposed to find methylated spirits or firestarter fuel? Another five minutes go by until a big bald guy wearing a puffed-up Arsenal jacket pulls his trolley and starts moving. Now I'm free and walking aimlessly and soon I find myself not too far from the tills.

There are long queues — hundreds trapped in lines that end at the checkout and start somewhere in the middle of the supermarket. There are many men and women dressed in Santa Claus outfits, walking along the lines, handing chocolate to those waiting. Whoever thought of this chocolate ruse, this little nod towards our humanity, is a genius.

And now I'm walking down a fast lane and the products turn into a white blur to my sides. I should stop someone from the staff and get directions but there's no way I'll be able to stop here so I keep walking, almost running, until against all odds a clearing, by the cereals, a space between people trying to rejoin the circulation and I shove my trolley and then myself and it's a tight space but big enough for one or two. Now I can breathe and watch the faces pass before me and feel nauseous.

I try to stop one of the Santa Clauses and miss him by an inch as I have to move my trolley just in time to stop a woman from taking the place I'm keeping for the clerk when I manage to stop one, thank you for shopping at Sainsbury's. Soon the woman is dragged by the flow and a she-Santa comes rushing in my direction. I grab her by the arm when she passes by and pull her to my side. She looks at me and smiles, I guess, for taking her out of that mess.

'Hi,' I say.

'Hello sir,' she says, 'Merry Christmas,' and she hands me a bonbon.

'Oh, thanks,' I say and put it in my pocket.

'How can I help you?' she asks.

'Methylated spirits? Do you know where I can find them?'

'Methylated spirits?'

'Yes, it's the liquid used to light the fondue oven, or whatever you call that thing.'

'Never heard of such a thing. Let me check with my manager,' she says and gets a walkie-talkie out of her pocket. She's pretty: brunette, delicate facial features under her Santa Claus beard. 'Barney… Stock enquiry… Over… Barney… He can't hear me,' she explains.

'It's OK. I'm not in a rush,' I say.

'Barney... Stock enquiry please... Over...'

'Reading you loud and clear... Over...' says Barney.

'Stock check, please... Over...'

'Go... Over...'

'Methylated spirits... Over...'

'Say again? Over...'

'Yes: methylated spirits. Mike-Echo-Tango...' I show her my list. 'Hotel-Yoke-Love-Alpha-Tango-Echo-Delta. Spirits, as in spirits. Got it? Over...'

'Mike-Echo-Tango-Hotel-Yoke-Love-Alpha-Tango-Echo-Delta, spirits? Over...'

'Affirmative.'

'Roger. Never heard of it. I'm checking the system now... Over...'

'Thanks. Over... He's checking.'

'Great,' I say. 'Busy?'

'Very busy,' she says, 'I apologise for the waiting times and the overcrowding and I would like to assure you that we are doing everything we can so that you have a great shopping experience.' She takes a breath of air. 'Merry Christmas,' she adds, and smiles.

'Merry Christmas, Virginia. Thanks for helping me, Virginia,' I say. She seems surprised that I know her name and then remembers that she's wearing a name badge and her face relaxes.

'It's OK. We're here to help,' she says. I think I blush. She looks in the other direction.

'Vee... Do you copy? Over...' interrupts Barney. She lifts the walkie-talkie.

'Reading you five Barney... Is it stocked? Over...'

'Negative… Over…'

'Can you try firestarter fuel? Over…'

'Sure… Firestarter as in fire starter? Over…'

'Yes… Over… Maybe we have more luck this time,' she says, Virginia.

'I appreciate your help, very much, Virginia,' I say and realise I like saying her name.

'Would you like another chocolate?' she asks.

'No, I'm OK, Virginia, I still have the other one.'

'OK.'

'Vee… Copy? Over…'

'Loud and clear… Over…'

'Also negative… Over…'

'Thanks Barney… Over…'

'Anything else, Vee? Over…' She looks at me. I move my head to indicate a 'no'.

'No, thanks, Barney… Over and out…'

'You're welcome… Over and out…'

'Sorry, sir. No luck.'

'No worries, Virginia.'

'Maybe you can find something round the cleaning products section…' she says. 'Something similar.'

'Thanks.'

'Or in the hardware shop next door.'

'I might try there,' I say. I don't want the conversation to end.

'Anything else sir?' I think for a couple of seconds but unfortunately can't think of anything.

'No. That's all.'

'OK. I have to go. Merry Christmas,' she says.

'Merry Christmas, Virginia,' I say. She smiles and then turns around and disappears into the fast lane.

I try to spot her in the flurry of people coming and going but I can't. She might have gone past me five thousand times already. She might have turned into particles.

The alcohol aisle. The smell coming from what could be broken bottles but could also be sweat. There are almost as many people here as there are near the tills. There are clerks everywhere and policemen carrying guns, ordering the lines of shoppers, directing them into the aisles, from either side into a sort of human funnel. Everything is incredibly efficient and the lines move fast and fearlessly. You can tell these people have been doing this for ages — it's in their DNA.

I stop in a clearing and study the situation with more attention. They step into the aisle and they walk fast and their hands move from the shelves to the trolley and from the trolley to the shelves with determination, while the bodies circulate in a never-ending stream. It reminds me of the Buddhists I saw walking around a praying wheel once in a temple in Kathmandu. They would touch this or that other bell, they would avoid touching other ones. A Knowledge illuminated their practice. I lacked it there and I lack it here. But these people have it, the Knowledge. There they knew which bell to touch and here they know if white wine follows cider, where whisky is located in relation to brandy. They can recognise the labels, the semiotic clues. Or maybe they just grab whatever they can.

And suddenly the unforeseen: a bottle falls and apologies for the waiting times, Merry Christmas, and keep moving waves one of the policemen, and everyone just walks over the broken glass. A deflated look on the dropper's face, for a millisecond, because he quickly grabs another bottle, and no longer looks deflated. At that moment I have my epiphany: obey the policemen, follow their gestures, get in, move fast, grab anything, and then get out on the other end of the boozing wheel. I rearrange my basket and zebra-coloured trolley; I will have to pull the trolley and carry the basket with the same hand. I'm ready.

I wait for the right moment while people of indeterminate class and age and gender pass before my eyes, leaving no space for me to join in. And then a guy with coiffured hair, brown furry anorak — there's a gap between him and a fat and slow guy wearing a tracksuit, walking behind him. When the first one passes by my side I squeeze after him. I can almost smell him. I CAN smell him — I can smell Kenzo for Men. And as we walk towards the booze 'I won't drop anything' I tell myself, and soon the policemen are just a couple of metres away, the one closer to me ordering people into lines, pointing the way with his Heckler & Koch MP5.

'Left. Right. Left. Right. Left. Left. Left. Right. Right. Left,' says the brave Authorised Firearm Officer, a huge guy with his cap all the way down to his eyes. 'Left,' he shouts at Kenzo for Men. 'Right!' I get. And I'm in.

The first bottles fly fast before my eyes and I don't grab any, too close for visibility, too many brands, too many colours, too many names for my culturally impaired eyes, thank you for shopping at Sainsbury's and Merry Christmas, and soon I've reached the end of the aisle boozeless and turn right, grab a bottle, the first that comes my way, and shove it into one of the side pockets of my trolley, and another right turn and two more bottles and cans, and when I'm halfway through the aisle I grab some more things of whatever and put the things of whatever in my basket and soon I'm out, moving towards distant aisles, walking until I find a quiet spot in the deserted world foods section.

I've managed to bag a bottle of sherry, two alcopops, four cans of weak lager, one rosé wine, and a half-litre bottle of dessert wine.

And now I've walked the aisle from end to end several times and there's no sign of anything remotely close to methylated spirits or firestarter fuel, no sign of anything flammable. I walk back to my trolley carrying a bag of toilet paper and kitchen rolls while I look around trying to identify the closest till. The closest one will have to do because I know for a fact that there won't be a less busy one.

There's a queue a few feet down. It's ridiculously long and the shoppers are queueing by the purposely empty shelves. I grab my basket and my trolley, look in both directions and rush towards the queue. When I get there I rest the basket on top of the trolley and soon I'm not the last one any longer: a blonde young woman stops behind me. She looks blushed — perhaps she's had a hard time looking for her own version of methylated spirits or firestarter fuel, or perhaps she's like that. Then I recognise Kenzo for Men in the line leading to the other till — he's red too. That's when I clock that everyone is red and that I'm feeling quite hot. Just to confirm my discovery, a metallic voice announces that Sainsbury's regrets to inform you that the ventilation system has stopped working but we would like to assure you that everything is being done to get it back on so that you have a great shopping experience, Merry Christmas! I take my jacket off and leave it hanging from my trolley. The others don't do the same as they're all carrying baskets. I feel a pang of seasonal solidarity and turn around.

'Do you want to rest your jacket here?' I ask the woman. She's wearing headphones, the white cables popping out of her ears and disappearing into her clothes.

'Sorry?'

'Do you want to rest your jacket here? It's hot.'

'I'm fine, thanks,' she says dismissively, and I feel stupid. I turn back to face the front of the queue. I feel a pat on my shoulder.

'You know… this is a baskets-only till,' she says, poker faced.

'Sorry?'

'Yes,' she says and points to a sign at the end of the aisle. It looks like a basket and has some letters that I can't read from here.

'Really?'

'Yes.'

'When I started queueing that sign wasn't visible,' I say.

'Sure,' she says and puts the headphones back on and looks at her phone.

I focus again on the sign. I can't really tell if it says it's for baskets only, but I'm certain that the drawing is a basket. And everyone around me only carries baskets. She must be right but I'm also right — I didn't see the sign when I joined the queue. She might have been here before, she must know the place. But I won't get out of the queue now that the tills are already in sight. I'm sure that this sign isn't valid on a day like today. She taps me on the back again.

'I think you should go to the other tills. You'll queue all the way to the front and then they'll send you somewhere else.'

'Thanks for your concern,' I say.

'It's unfair,' she says.

'I might have fewer things than you anyway!' I say, looking at her basket, overflowing with sweets and Nurofen and little things in small plastic bags, each a different purple hue.

'That's not the point,' she says. 'I've got a basket. This queue is for baskets only,' she says.

'I'm not going anywhere,' I say but I can't be sure if she hears me or not because once more she's wearing her headphones and staring at the light in the palm of her hand.

By now the other people in the queue are aware of our conversation. I can feel their red faces staring in my direction. It's tense and I should go but I won't. I'll queue all the way up to the tills and if I have to go somewhere else afterwards, I'll go. Another tap on my shoulder and I turn around with hatred bursting through my eyes.

'Hi,' says Virginia, with her Santa beard pulled under her chin.

'Oh, hi!' I say.

'Did you have any luck with what was it?

'Methylated spirits or firestarter fuel?'

'Yes.'

'No luck,' I say.

'Well, try the hardware shop.'

'I'll do that.'

'Would you like a bonbon?'

'Sure,' I say. 'Thanks a lot!'

'My pleasure.' She passes me a bonbon and I put it in my pocket, where I put the other one earlier.

'Can I ask you something, Virginia?'

'Sure,' she says and smiles.

'I've just realised that I'm in the wrong queue. Apparently this one is for baskets only.' Virginia looks at the end of the line. 'I couldn't see the sign when I started queueing. It was too far away,' I say.

'Oh!' she says.

'It's not my fault,' I say.

'It's not your fault,' she agrees.

'Because this lady here is adamant that I'm in the wrong queue,' I say and nod towards the woman, who pretends she's not listening.

'Where did you start queueing?' asks Virginia.

'Over there,' I point. 'At the very end of this aisle, by the toilet paper.'

Virginia walks to end of the line, when she gets there she points to an imaginary space with both her index fingers. I give her a thumbs up. She looks in the sign's direction. Then comes back to my spot.

'It's true. There's no angle,' she says. 'Stay in this queue. I'll tell the cashier.'

'You're amazing! Thanks a lot Virginia.'

'You're welcome,' she says.

'Great,' I say.

'Would you like another bonbon?'

'Sure. Thanks,' I say.

'There you go. Merry Christmas.'

'Merry Christmas, Virginia.'

'Great. I need to get going,' she says.

'Right. Thanks for your help.'

'I'll tell the cashier now to let you go through.'

'Thanks. Zebra pattern,' I say pointing at my trolley. 'Unmissable.'

'True,' she says and chuckles. 'Bye!'

'Bye, Virginia...' She walks away. I watch her disappear towards the tills. I turn around to face the woman behind me.

'Did you hear what she said?' She takes her headphones off.

'What?'

'Yes. Did you hear that? She said that I can stay in this queue.'

'Sorry. I wasn't listening.'

'I think you were listening.'

'Whatever,' she says. I don't answer back.

The guy before has placed several bags of peanuts on the belt, more than ten, we would like to assure you that we are doing everything we can to fix the ventilation system, Merry Christmas! Peanuts, only peanuts. The belt moves a few millimetres forward. I start unloading my shopping in the free space, a couple of bottles that I lay horizontally. When the belt moves again the bottles rattle. He turns back to look at them. I continue pulling things from my trolley. He seems irritated — he looks at my dessert wine and my alcopops with anxiety. Suddenly he moves forward and gets a plastic divider and shoves it in between my bottles and his peanuts. Then he looks at me. I don't look back at him and just continue to unload. The belt continues to move and I slowly finish emptying my trolley. A couple of minutes pass in which the belt doesn't move. Then it moves just a little bit and then it stops again. I hear huffing and I raise my head. The guy is tapping his feet on the ground, the old woman before him has stopped bagging her items. The cashier is looking around with a concerned expression. There are some blue lights flashing on top of the till.

'The till system is down. It'll only be a couple of minutes. Apologies for any inconvenience caused!' she says. The guy huffs and I huff too and the old woman at the front huffs too and the woman behind me huffs as well. The cashier stands up from her seat and looks around. She waves her hands in the air towards the end of the checkouts. 'Sorry!' she says to the old woman and then sinks back into her seat. I get my phone out and check the time: it's late, the hardware shop must have closed already. What will happen if the system can't be fixed? There's no way I'll go back to the end of the queue. I'll probably just walk away with an empty trolley. I put my phone back in my pocket and get my hand dirty with the melted chocolate, from the three bonbons, now an amorphous mass. I get the blob out of my pocket and throw it on the floor: it explodes into a brown stain.

Time does what time does and nothing really changes but the fact that we are two minutes older. The lights keep flashing and the cashier keeps moving her head in every direction. I feel sorry for her because it looks as if her head could become unscrewed from her neck. She seems pretty much near meltdown and I wouldn't be surprised if she started crying and walked out of her job, thank you for shopping at Sainsbury's, Merry Christmas! But I can't help huffing in unison with everybody else. And to make matters worse I can feel Peanut Man inspecting my things, again. He won't stop glaring over my products. At first I thought it was paranoia, the unfounded suspicion that I might want to get him to pay for my things, but now I realise his is simply the lowest and most mundane form of resentment. I can feel his eyes going over my stuff. Stopping at the olive oil. Jumping to my Dijon mustard. Moving towards the washing-up tablets. Coming back to the alcopops. The olives. The grisini. Chicken. Salmon. Perhaps he's mentally calculating my bill. Perhaps he sees me as the paroxysm of the Metropolitan Elite. God knows what he's thinking but I can tell he hates me. Suddenly the lights stop flashing.

A chubby guy in a Santa costume is standing next to our cashier now. He's touching the screen. Our cashier seems more relaxed. He gets a set of keys from somewhere below his huge Santa belly and inserts them next to the printer. A loud noise and the belt advances a couple of centimetres. I feel like cheering — everyone must but nobody does.

'Thanks Barney,' says the cashier. Thanks Barney.

'You're welcome,' says Barney and he walks away, in his Santa outfit, a hero without a cape.

The cashier goes back to her normal position, the products fly from her hands to the ramp and from the ramp to the polyethylene bags and the belt moves and the system is functional again and I pull my basket from the depths below the till, and I gradually empty it, oblivious to Peanut Man, and soon the old woman pays and leaves. Charging ten bags of peanuts mustn't be that hard as I'm soon facing the cashier.

'Hi. Merry Christmas. Thanks for waiting and apologies for the delay,' she says.

'Merry Christmas. Don't worry. I've got a trolley,' I say. 'Is that OK? Virginia said it was OK.' She gets up slightly from her seat and checks my trolley out.

'Oh, it's you,' she says and smiles. 'Yes, it's fine! Don't worry. She said the sign wasn't visible from the start of the queue, right?'

'Exactly. Thanks a lot,' I say and I turn around to face the woman behind me: she's gone.

'No problem,' says the cashier and starts moving my shopping over the laser. 'Do you need any bags?'

'Just one or two,' I say.

'Sure,' she says. 'Nice trolley.'

'Thanks!' I say.

She seems quite happy. She must be heat-struck in that costume but she's happy.

Wine. Chicken. Mustard, Dijon. Tuna. Olives. From her hands to the ramp into the trolley. Heavies always go at the bottom; lights on top. Eggs will be waiting for a while, to go on top of everything else. Toilet paper and kitchen rolls in bags, hanging from the side, rattling noiselessly all the way home. And so on and everything must end and soon I'm finishing my packing. Before putting away the Italian antipasti selection I fan my face with it.

'It's so hot in here,' I say.

'Terribly hot,' she says. 'Have you got a Nectar card?' she asks, smiling.

'Nope. Sorry.' I always say sorry.

'It's two-hundred and eighty-four, fifty-eight,' she says and I shove my Visa Debit in the card reader. 'Thanks for shopping at Sainsbury's, have a Merry Christmas,' she says, scratching her Santa beard.

'Merry Christmas,' I say. And then I walk out into the cold.

BARBECUE AND EXHUMATION IN VICTORIA PARK VILLAGE

It's a house near Victoria Park Village, 'where Hackney looks nicer', The Landlady said over the phone without a hint of irony, and I didn't have much trouble locating the address with the map I drew from the internet because I have no printer and I didn't want to walk around the area with my phone in my hand, now that moped thieves are a thing. I look around for a while, taking in the beautiful road, the smell of lavender coming from the plants, the sounds of children laughing in the distance, the complete absence of car alarms or police sirens — it's a beautiful day.

I walk. And then I stop walking.

And soon I'm ringing the bell in the house that could be the house on either side or across the road, save for that little number nailed to the door: sixty-nine. I pick up the plant from the floor after arranging my shirt and fix a broad smile on my face. A couple of minutes elapse, my face begins to stiffen and the door remains closed. I leave the plant once more on the floor and ring the bell again. I pick up the plant after rearranging my shirt and the smile. Half a minute or so later The Landlady opens the door. She's holding a glass of rosé and wearing a pair of Wayfarers, just like mine but they look better on her, they make more sense on her, they look like she's not trying.

'Oh, hello! Do come in, please,' says The Landlady. 'Wayfarers! Love them.'

'Thanks,' I say. 'You've got them too!'

'Yes I do!' She sounds excited.

'I've got some food and drinks — and I bought you a plant too.'

'Oh, thanks. You shouldn't have bothered!' She looks at the plant.

'I wasn't sure if you liked plants or not…'

'Oh, it's perfectly fine! I love plants. Wait until you see my back garden. It's a nice plant. What is it?'

'A potus.'

'Putus? Never heard of it! Anyway, come in, do come in!'

I come in.

It's a disproportionally narrow but long house, a planning aberration, probably resulting from one house having been turned into two in order to maximise profit. There's light at the back and music too. The Landlady leads the way and I follow behind. We get to a tiny kitchen and I leave the beers and the sausages on the table. It's still sunny outside and Richard Hawley is playing through the stereo, singing that tonight the streets are ours, a good omen, even if this is about a garden and a barbecue.

'Where should I leave the plant?'

'Put it anywhere. Can I get you some wine or a beer?' asks The Landlady. 'But you drink wine, don't you? You must drink wine…'

'Beer is fine. Thanks.'

'Ah, OK!'

The Landlady opens a tiny fridge that looks like a hotel mini-bar and gets a can of Stella. I open it and before drinking from it raise the can to toast with her.

'Cheers.'

'Cheers.'

'Is it a tradition that you people bring plants when you're invited to a party?' she asks.

'Sorry?'

'Yes. Is it a tradition? You seemed very attentive to all plant matters. Is this something you people do, taking plants to places?'

'I just thought it would be nice to bring a plant.'

'So, you don't always take plants whenever you're invited somewhere?'

'Not really.'

'That's so sweet,' she says. 'That you brought that plant just for me.'

'Oh, it's nothing!'

'No, really. Thanks a lot: it's a lot — it means a lot. It really does, especially in the times we live. Thank you very much!'

'You're welcome. Thanks for inviting me!'

'Oh, don't say, don't say! Anyway… Come and meet the rest of the gang!'

People in the garden, all wearing Wayfarers, like The Landlady and I. A tiny stair, just two or three steps and the grass at our feet. A smoking barbecue with sausages, burgers and some red and green peppers.

'Everyone: this is The Tenant.'

'Hi!' says everyone.

'This is The Former Banker,' says The Landlady and points to the guy working the grill.

'Hi,' says The Former Banker.

'Hi,' I say.

'That's The Former Banker's Writer Wife,' says The Landlady.

'Hi,' I say.

'Hi,' says The Former Banker's Writer Wife.

'And that one over there is The Unhappy Estate Agent,' says The Landlady.

'Hi,' says The Unhappy Estate Agent.

'Nice to meet you,' I say.

'Have a seat,' says The Landlady and I sit on a reclining chair by the barbecue. All the smoke is coming my way and soon I will be stinking of pork sausage but it's too late to change seats: it could be deemed an infringement of etiquette. I have a drink from my can of Stella — at least the beer is cold.

'So what do you do?' asks The Former Banker.

'Sorry?' I ask.

'Yeah. What do you do for a living?'

'Oh. I work for University College London.'

'Are you a Literature Professor?' asks The Former Banker's Writer Wife.

'No. Admin staff. I work in the Registry. Very unliterary.'

'Oh, I see,' says The Former Banker's Writer Wife.

'How long have you been here?' asks The Unhappy Estate Agent.

'In London?'

'Yes.'

'Fourteen years. And a half. Almost fifteen years, actually.'

'Wow! That's a long time!' says The Landlady.

'Are you on a work visa?' asks The Former Banker.

'No, Italian passport. But I became British last year...'

'Oh, I see. I thought you needed a visa anyway,' says The Former Banker's Writer Wife.

'You don't need a visa if you've got a European passport,' says The Unhappy Estate Agent. 'Not at the moment, not until they have a clearer idea of what will happen.'

'No one knows what will happen... How do you feel about all this, you know? Do you want to go back home? Do you hate us?' — The Former Banker's Writer Wife.

'Oh, please! Stop grilling him!' says The Landlady.

'It's fine,' I say. 'I don't think much will happen, to be fair.'

'Someone will have to get deported,' says The Unhappy Estate Agent. 'It'll destroy the housing market and—'

'He's also a part-time vocational writer,' says The Landlady, addressing The Former Banker's Writer Wife.

'Really?' asks the latter.

'Well, I like writing,' I say.

'Are you a published author?' asks The Unhappy Estate Agent.

'No. Not yet.'

'What do you write?' asks The Former Banker's Writer Wife.

'Fiction.'

'Novel or short stories?'

'Short stories. But nothing serious.'

'As a fiction writer you're only as good as your first

novel,' says The Former Banker's Writer Wife. 'Why don't you write one?'

'The Landlady mentioned he's only a part-time vocational writer,' replies The Former Banker, defending me, I guess.

'Yes, she did. It doesn't matter, I want to know,' says his wife, a bit cross. 'I'm a published author — I published a chapbook last year,' she adds.

'Nice!' I say and sip some more beer.

'Poetry. Non-rhyming. Experimental.'

'Oh, great,' I say. 'Where can I get it?'

'I'll get you a copy,' she says. 'I've got some copies here with me. Remind me later.'

'I will.'

'Only fifteen pounds,' says The Former Banker.

'No problem.'

'So, how's the flat?' asks The Landlady.

'Oh, very well. Although the boiler is still a bit noisy.'

'I thought they had fixed that!'

'They came over, but they didn't really fix the problem.'

'My mother went with the engineers,' The Landlady says to the others. 'She loves it when I give her these little tasks.'

'How cute,' says The Former Banker's Writer Wife.

'Yes. She told me a nice European-looking brunette girl opened the door,' The Landlady says, with faux complicity.

'Oh, yes. My friend Vanja. I had to go to work but she stayed over to open the door for your mum.'

'Have you got a European girlfriend?' asks The Former Banker's Writer Wife. 'Is she Eastern European?'

'She's just a good friend!'

'He he,' laughs The Former Banker.

'Where is she from?' asks The Former Banker's Writer Wife.

'Slovakia.'

'So she is Eastern European! I knew it! Poor her... She must be really worried. Really really worried.'

'Anyway, I'm disappointed that they didn't fix the boiler,' interrupts The Landlady. 'I'll get the engineers to check it again; perhaps another engineer. Any ideas?' she asks The Unhappy Estate Agent.

'I'll get you my man's number,' says The Unhappy Estate Agent without lowering his head, now pointed upwards in the sun's direction.

'Perfect, I'll speak to Mum and see when she's free.'

'Thanks,' I say.

'The door,' says The Former Banker.

'Really?' asks The Landlady.

'Yes, I think I've heard the door,' I say, trying to be useful.

The landlady pours some more rosé wine into her glass and leaves. I have another sip from my can.

'Are you writing anything at the moment?' asks The Former Banker's Writer Wife.

'Not at the moment,' I say.

'Why?'

'I can't find the time.'

'You must MAKE the time,' she says. 'YOU MUST. If you take writing seriously YOU MUST find the time. Even if it means destroying the rest of your life in the process.' I don't reply but I nod in agreement.

Some voices from inside the house. The Landlady is leading a chubby short woman and a tall dark-haired corpulent guy. 'Come in. Come in! Do welcome The Boring Civil Servant and The Common Unemployed Boyfriend!'

'Hello, everyone. Nice to see you!' says The Boring Civil Servant.

'Hello!' says The Common Unemployed Boyfriend.

Everyone says hi, different variations, same message.

'This is The Tenant,' says The Landlady. I move my head up and down once more, with a big grin on my face.

'Hi,' says The Boring Civil Servant.

'Hi,' says The Common Unemployed Boyfriend. He sits next to me. We're both drinking Stella. 'Nice day, mate. Lovely weather!'

'Yes! We don't get many days like this,' I say.

'Where are you from?' asks The Common Unemployed Boyfriend.

'Argentina.'

'Cool! Never been there. Is it nice?'

'It's fine. Nice weather.'

'Is it cheap?'

'Quite cheap. Depends on the inflation and the exchange rate.'

'Gotta go there. Once I was in Amsterdam.'

'I've never been to Amsterdam.'

'You've gotta go. Nice place, nice beer, nice food, nice birds, nice skunk.'

'Nice.'

'Outside the M25 is generally better, don't you think?' he asks. 'Not too up north, though. Up north they'd probably lynch you, mate.'

And so on.

The garden is narrow and long, like a negative copy of the built part of the house. There's a huge tree at the back, with hanging branches and leaves covering at least a fifth of the space. The houses on either side are hidden behind tall and twisted wooden walls. Voices can be heard, people chatting behind these walls, some traces of accented English, music. And there's smoke — everybody seems to be out in the gardens grilling something. I look around and then up to the sun — it's a pleasant moment, I guess.

'Do you smoke?' asks The Common Unemployed Boyfriend. 'I mean weed.'

'Yeah, sometimes.'

'We'll roll up then.'

'Great,' I say.

'Later. Gotta eat something first. Darling, get us a bite, will you?'

'Do you want a sausage, darling?' asks The Boring Civil Servant.

'Yes, darling.'

'Salad, darling?'

'No salad, darling.'

'What about you? Sorry, I forgot your name…'

'He's The Tenant,' says The Landlady.

'I'm fine,' I say. 'I'll get some drinks. Can I get anyone anything?'

'Get us another Stella,' says The Common Unemployed Boyfriend. Nobody else replies.

'I'll go with you,' says The Landlady. 'I have to stop for a wee.' The Former Banker's Writer Wife seems to find this statement funny.

We walk up the tiny stairs and into the kitchen. The Landlady opens the fridge and pours some wine into her glass. She closes the fridge and pumps up the music's volume.

'Oh, sorry. I forgot to get your beers,' she says. 'Help yourself; I'm going to the loo. Wait for me here, please. Don't go!'

I open the fridge and get the two beers and lean against the counter. I open the can and have a sip. I look around the kitchen and there isn't anything significant to catch my attention, save a surprisingly tacky set of curtains and a small statue of a frog. I look towards the garden and spot The Common Unemployed Boyfriend looking my way. The Common Unemployed Boyfriend gives me two thumbs up and signals for me to throw the beer. I throw it and the beer flies all the way to his hands. Two thumbs up once more and a wink. The Common Unemployed Boyfriend opens the can of beer and it squirts; he laughs. The rest of the guests stare at him and then at me. And then they keep talking among themselves. I drink some more beer and feel I'm beginning to get light-headed.

Arctic Monkeys or some indie band. I don't particularly like indie music — never got it. I go to the stereo, stashed in a corner next to some fruits and vegetables and a pile of CDs — some people still keep their CDs. I lean towards them and scan through the names: Interpol, Blur, Stereophonics, Pulp, Sonic Youth, Asteroid No. Four, Gorillas, Groove Armada. A tap on my right shoulder. I stand up and The Landlady is smiling at me with a broad drunken smile.

'I was an indie girl,' she says.

'I see,' I say. 'I would never have imagined it!'

'Ha ha. Yes. Young rebellious years. I even went to Glasto a couple of times.'

'Really?'

'Yes. Do you know Glasto? Glastonbury. It's a big music festival. Have you heard about it?'

'I think so...'

'It's in Somerset... Somewhere, not in London... Many many bands, you sleep in a tent, share stinking toilets... It rains all the time. It's great!'

'I think I know which one.'

'Wellies... You know these rubber boots? Like farmer boots? Do you know those?'

'Yes,' I say.

'Drugs, booze... You go to the toilet in holes in the ground in which five thousand people went before... It's full of guys trying to spike your drinks...'

'Sounds extreme.'

'It's fun,' she says. 'We were saying the other day, with The Former Banker and his Writer Wife, that we should go again, maybe next year. Maybe you want to come!'

'Sounds good. Let's see closer to the date.'

'Sure. You should deffo come. They're bringing their children. It will be fun.'

'Oh, I didn't know they had children.'

'Yes. Three: one, two and three years old.' She stumbles and leans against the counter, close to me.

'Nice. It's like a ladder — one, two, three.'

'Ha ha. Yes, One of them, the youngest, is slightly stupid, though.'

'Oh...'

'Yes. She's been depressed. That's why she started to write poetry.'

'They say it helps.'

'He lost his job a while back and never found a new one. I think he started the banking crisis.'

'Which crisis?' I ask.

'This crisis we're in now. We've been in a financial crisis for like nine years!'

'Are we still in that crisis? I thought we were in a new crisis now,' I say.

'It's all part of the same crisis from nine years ago… It all boils down to that, that's what they say. Anyway… They might have to sell the house. They've already sold one of the cars. They might have to put their kids in a state school. It's critical. But we are deffo going to Glasto, next year. Think about it.'

'I will.'

'Anyway… Speaking of them: sorry if they ask too many questions! They want to know you. I spoke a lot about you!'

'You did?'

'Yes.'

'Thank you.' We stare at each other in silence. 'I'll get some more beers to spare me the trip,' I say to break it.

'Good thinking!'

'Shall I top you up?'

'Yes, fill me up please.'

We go back to the garden and sit in our chairs.

'I've got you another beer,' I say to The Common Unemployed Boyfriend.

'You're a genius, mate!' he says. The Former Banker's Writer Wife stares at us, The Landlady smiles, The Former

Banker is still cooking the sausages, while The Boring Civil Servant and The Unhappy Estate Agent converse towards the end of the garden. 'Say matey, how do you like it here?'

'Do you mean in London?'

'Yeah.'

'I like it. I've been here like fifteen years already.'

'That's a long time.'

'Yeah, pretty long.'

'You must really like it, then.'

'Yes, I do.'

'How come you are here if you are from Argentina? Can you come and work and live here?'

'I came on an Italian passport.'

'Oh, I see! Will they be sending you back home?'

'I'm British now.'

'Really?'

'Yes!'

'For how long?'

'Last year, November, maybe. I can't remember.'

'See, what I find incredible about you people, I mean you people not from here, is how you come here, make this place your home, learn the language, get a job. It's like you've come from here, more or less. Some people don't like it and want to get you deported, I mean not you, but you know what I mean… But I quite like people coming here and all that. You know what I mean? You know that's how I feel, don't you?'

'Yes.'

'I think it's great, mate. I'm happy for you, happy that now you're one of us,' he says and raises his hand to get a high five from me and I comply with the request. 'I say it's about time we rolled a spliff… What do you say?'

'Yeah, it's a good time now. I'll just have a puff. I'm a bit tipsy already.'

'Oh, don't be a ponce, mate! You'll be fine. Summer, sun and all that.'

The Common Unemployed Boyfriend gets a small bag of tobacco and a packet of large blue Rizlas out of his pocket. 'Surprise,' he says and he shows me a yellow container, from a Kinder Egg, which he shakes and then opens. He leaves the two sides of the container on top of the tobacco bag, itself on his lap, and then gets a cigarette paper out from the packet. He throws in some tobacco and plenty of ground skunk. He works on the spliff with admirable concentration and in less than a minute he has finished rolling a beautiful joint, the size of a small cigar. He lights up, drags a few times and then passes me the joint and I puff on it a couple of times and then pass it back to The Common Unemployed Boyfriend. He has a few more drags.

'Want to smoke?' he asks the group. The Landlady is the only one to nod — she stretches her arm, gets hold of the joint and drags once. She coughs a couple of times, drinks some wine and then she continues to talk with The Former Banker's Writer Wife, holding the joint between her right index and middle finger. The Common Unemployed Boyfriend and I stare at her hand for a couple of minutes, until she puffs on it once more and then passes it back to me and I puff on it and then pass it to The Common Unemployed Boyfriend who has a few drags and skips The Landlady to give it back to me (I'm still holding the smoke from the previous round). I smoke again and gesture to give the joint back to The Common Unemployed Boyfriend who signals — with the universal up-down hand movement —

for me to slow down. So I drag once more and feel my throat a bit dry and have a drink from my can of Stella. And then I smoke once more, have one more drink, and pass the spliff back to The Common Unemployed Boyfriend.

The beer is so cold, so nice and cold.

'Shall I get two more beers?' I ask.

'Mate, you talk so much sense!' says The Common Unemployed Boyfriend and goes back to the joint. He goes for it and then moves his arm forward to pass it back to me. I gesture no no no, enough.

'Anyone? Drinks?'

Nobody replies. The Common Unemployed Boyfriend put his right index and right thumb together and moves the hand up and down, calling everybody a bunch of wankers. Nobody but The Boring Civil Servant and I spot him. She gives him an evil look and I laugh. When I stand up and walk towards the kitchen I realise that I'm pretty drunk and stoned. The kitchen is only a few metres away but it takes me ages to make it there, like a human Zeno's paradox. But I do get there, and then to the toilet, after a jump cut. Lid up and an eternal piss. Lid down, flush and out. I succeed in not looking at my face in the mirror. Another jump cut and I'm in the kitchen once more. I get two cans from the fridge and go back to the garden.

'You've left your fly down,' says The Common Unemployed Boyfriend and I look at my crotch. 'I'm taking the piss! Thanks,' he says when he gets the beer. 'Good shit, innit.'

'Pretty strong. I'm quite stoned.'

'Good skunk. GM Dutch — we'll miss this shit, I'm telling you.'

'I'm having time troubles,' I say.

'Uh?'

'Yes. It's like time is flexible. It took me forever to go to the kitchen. And then I was in the toilet just like that and I pissed forever. Do you know what I mean?'

'Yeah… Sort of…'

'Quite scary.'

'You'll be fine. Just don't fight it, mate: be with the wave.'

It's so sunny still. If only the walls around the garden were lower — the sun only succeeds in bathing us from the chest up and I feel half cold and half hot. But it's nice anyway. And birds chirping and indie bands playing from bluetooth speakers connected to iPhones, iPads, MacBooks. Moments of beauty — Instagram moments — make them last, make time stretch, let a minute become five minutes and five minutes twenty-five hours and so on. And I'm holding the beer in my right hand, forever staring at the others, listening to their talk about remortgaging houses, breastfeeding, Glasto, the coming elections and not voting Tory even if Labour are shit — perhaps they'll vote Green or LibDem. Well-informed people, educated, lovely accents, multi-cultured, left-leaning now, to the centre by their mid-forties, age fifty-five and above they'll buy the *Times* but they'll never read the *Mail*, no, not them. How beautiful, young and English they are — I love them. Does this mark the beginning of a new era? Me being among the English? I'm certainly among them, sharing their back garden, eating their sausages, listening to their music, their talk, answering their questions, drinking their drink and getting inebriated with their culture, still in their country, one of the ones who are allowed to stay, not like the others who'll leave, the ones who have left and the ones who never made it or were never welcomed. I never dreamed about this. I never thought I would make it this far. I'm one of them now — this integration bliss is amazing. Stretch the duration, make it last and drink some more beer. Avoid jump cuts of any kind. Be here. Be with the wave, like he said, until the wave passes. Extend this moment forever. And smile: I smile at them and I smile at The Landlady. She smiles back at me.

'Would you get me a glass of wine?' she asks, slurring a bit.

'Sure,' I say and go back to the kitchen, walking very slowly, step after step. I can hear them laughing behind my back but I don't care. It's Sunday and it's sunny. Plus, she's slurring and I'm not.

'There you go,' I say and pass her a glass of rosé, just some minutes or decades later, perhaps at an earlier moment, I don't know.

'Thanks,' she says.

'You have a lovely backyard,' I say.

'A bit small.'

'It's nice.'

'I'm glad you like it. And I'm glad you came.'

'Yeah, I'm glad I came.'

'Are you having a good time?'

'Yeah.'

'Can you follow our conversations?'

'Yes.'

'Don't we talk too fast for you?'

'It's fine, really.'

'He's got a funny accent, doesn't he?' she points to The Common Unemployed Boyfriend.

'The finest of Plaistow,' says The Common Unemployed Boyfriend smiling back at her.

'What is that?' jokes The Landlady, pretending not to understand.

'Pure East End. Born and bred.'

'Don't worry if you don't understand. I don't understand him myself,' she says.

'I do understand him,' I say.

'The guy is a star!' says The Common Unemployed Boyfriend. High five.

'Where did you learn English again?' she asks.

'At school.'

'I thought they taught French in school,' she says.

'They teach English back home.'

'That's brilliant,' she says.

'Yes, it is,' I say.

And then it's already quite dark.

We've moved to the back of the garden and we're sitting under the tree. Everyone is still wearing their shades and drinking. The Common Unemployed Boyfriend and I have to be the drunkest but The Landlady is quite drunk too. The Unhappy Estate Agent disappeared a while ago, citing an urgent matter pertaining to some flat in London Fields. And The Former Banker, his wife and the other two women are talking — animated words that make no sense at all, slurred words, careless sunny Sunday words that I attempt and fail to retain. More of the same but somehow different, an exhaustion of the usual themes — sunny Sunday variations.

Yes, I love Fleetwood Mac. You backdate at least thirty years with your musical taste, honey. Don't be a bitch, please. Ha, ha. Stevie Nicks — now, that's a woman. You're making your wife jealous! Let him be — I'll take the only car he's got left when we get divorced! Ha ha. Anyway. Nice weather isn't it? Don't you wish it stayed like this forever? Oh, poor you... It can't last forever. It will start raining any moment. We haven't been blessed with a proper summer, have we? Are you having one of your days? Been having them forever darling! I think you're turning menopausal. Ha ha. Talking about the weather, when I go back to work —if I go back, ha ha — we're thinking of having a holiday in Amalfi. Where's that? I think it's the south of Italy — it's somewhere in Europe, anyway. Have you been to Ibiza? That's not Italy. Yes, I know but it's still awesome. No way, it's full of junkies and gays. You live surrounded by junkies anyway, and far from the beach. But I've got Victoria Park. Sod that park, you need to move to South London — much greener. No way, I'd rather live in East Berlin, I mean, if we still could. It's all the same now. Yes, it's all the same. LOL (someone actually says 'lol'). And so on and so on. Talk, talk, sunny Sunday talk.

'That's it, matey,' slurs The Common Unemployed Boyfriend. 'You gotta do what you gotta do. You can't do otherwise. Or you'll be fucked. You know what I mean.'

'Yes. True,' I slur.

'After all a man's a man. If you can't be a man you're nothing. You know what I mean. You gotta do what you gotta do.'

'True.'

'There's plenty of fish in the sea. If there's anything in the sea it's fish. And water. There's a lot of water. But it's fish that we're talking about, and it's full of it. Fucking bitch; don't worry about her. Get another one. I'm with you, buddy!' High five.

'Thanks… yes.'

'High five.'

'High five,' I say and we high five again but I don't have a clue what he's talking about.

'I'm glad you're here, matey. These bunch of cunts are a pain in the arse. Wow, said it! Hahahaha. Fleetwood Mac! Ibiza! Go back to fucking Chiswick! Hahahahaha!' he gives them the two fingers. 'Ha ha ha ha!' They laugh too.

'Common Unemployed Boyfriend!' says The Boring Civil Servant, reprimanding him. The Common Unemployed Boyfriend pulls a face and they all laugh but it's clear he thinks they're all a bunch of cunts and it's clear that they know he thinks they're a bunch of cunts. And he may as well be right.

'This happens when you befriend the plebs,' says The Former Banker and they laugh, everyone laughs. The Common Unemployed Boyfriend laughs and I laugh too although I don't really know why I'm laughing because it wasn't that good a joke. But they're all laughing and so it's my duty to laugh too. And we're all quite drunk, so laughter comes naturally. And I wouldn't like to be an alien to this laughter because it's so contagious and I feel that this laughter is mine as well and I have a right to laugh.

'I'm joking,' says The Common Unemployed Boyfriend. 'You know I love you all!'

'We love you too!' says The Landlady. 'And you too, The Tenant. We love you too!'

'I think your opinion is slightly biased,' says The Former Banker's Writer Wife.

'How dare you!' says The Landlady and the laughter escalates once more.

'The chicken's ready!' says The Common Unemployed Boyfriend and he elbows me. 'Ha ha! The chicken is sooooo ready,' he says again. 'Someone will skewer the chicken tonight! Who will skewer the chicken? Who will skewer the chicken, UH?' he asks and elbows me again.

'Stop it,' says The Landlady and she blushes and they all laugh and laugh and laugh and I may be laughing too and some more drink, some more talk. The Amateur Footballer Admin moved in with his Aspiring Media Whore Girlfriend. The Gay Lawyer bought a flat in Walthamstow. The Asian British Guy With a Rich Father has moved to Australia (or was it Singapore?) and he's taking over some family business. How long since we finished uni? I've never been to uni! Darling, you didn't even get your A-levels! Laughter. LAUGHTER.

And I listen carefully but I miss most of the conversation. I won't speak and I won't even attempt to open my mouth. Not because I'm angry or sulking about something and I hate them and wish they were dead, that I had never come. It has more to do with a sudden loss of speech provoked by the necessity to keep some kind of contact with the situation — a matter of prioritising energies. No more words for me for a while.

It's getting colder: dew, chills.

'Shall I brew something?' asks someone.

'That sounds like a good idea,' replies someone else.

Now next to the grill, something is burning, intentionally. I must have fallen asleep a couple of seconds ago. When I open my eyes The Landlady is saying something. She's speaking to me. I nod and laugh but actually don't get a word of what she says. She repeats it and I laugh again and then she moves closer and kisses me. I feel her lips first and then her teeth and finally her tongue. She must smell like booze but I can't tell because I must smell like booze too, because my mouth tastes like booze. I automatically thrust my hand forward and place it on her leg. She stops kissing me. I move my hand back. And she kisses me again — it's a nice kiss. I enjoy it. I move forward to kiss her and she moves her head out of the way. She laughs aloud, teases me, then reaches for the wine glass and has a sip. And then kisses me once more and with admirable aim spits the wine in my mouth. I drink it, it's only rosé after all. I get turned on by this and thrust my hand forward once more and rest it on her leg and she stops again.

'Have some more beer,' she says.

'I'm fine,' I say.

'No, really. Have some beer: you have bad breath.'

'OK,' I say and drink some more beer from my can and she kisses me again.

'Do you want to come inside?'

'Would you let me come inside?'

'Don't be silly! It's getting cold here.'

I look around. 'Where's the rest?'

'Everybody's gone.'

'Really?'

'Yes.'

'When did they leave?' I slur.

'Two hours ago.'

'Ha ha. Nah…'

'Yes. I told you already. Have some more beer and let's go inside: I'm cold.'

'Yes, let me come inside.'

'Stop it! Let's go inside.'

'Let's stay here a bit longer…'

'I'm cold!'

Now back under the tree at the back. It's dark, almost completely dark. The Landlady is telling a story about a holiday in the Lake District and how it rained all the time, 'It was like *Withnail and I* with sex,' she says. They all laugh. Weren't they gone? Anyway. Meanwhile, I'm staring at what seems to be a small tombstone in a corner, next to a rosemary plant. I can't see the words written on the tombstone but I'm quite sure it's a tombstone. A tiny tombstone, a pet's tombstone.

'Yeah, it's a tombstone,' says The Landlady, intercepting my gaze. I don't reply and just smile back at her.

'Fuck,' says The Common Unemployed Boyfriend, 'you've got a tombstone in the garden!'

'Yep, she's got a tombstone in the garden…' says The Former Banker.

'Skeletons in the closet, tombstones in the garden,' says The Former Banker's Writer Wife.

'Never saw it before,' says The Common Unemployed Boyfriend.

'Me neither,' says The Boring Civil Servant. 'What is it?'

'My grandpa, Fonzie,' says The Landlady and they all laugh.

'Shit, I wonder what it is...' says The Common Unemployed Boyfriend.

'Not a clue!' says The Landlady. 'It came with the house. Nineteen eighty-four, nineteen eighty-nine...'

'Sounds like a badger to me,' says The Former Banker.

'Badger? Who has a badger, darling?'

'I had a pet badger when I was a kid!' says The Former Banker.

'You were a strange kid,' says his wife and they all laugh. I follow the conversation closely. I understand that they are talking about the tombstone but I don't have a clue what a badger is.

'I think it's a fish,' says The Boring Civil Servant. 'They live for four or five years.'

'Would you bury a fish?' says The Former Banker. 'I mean... I think people just flush dead fish down the toilet...'

'Yeah, I think he's right,' says The Common Unemployed Boyfriend.

'Flush it?' asks The Landlady.

'Yes! Where else?'

'You're sick!' she says. 'That's so cruel!' They all laugh.

'Why don't we just dig it out?' says The Former Banker's Writer Wife.

'Are you joking?' asks The Boring Civil Servant.

'No, let's dig it out.'

'I don't think we should,' says The Former Banker. 'Just leave the thing there.'

'What do you think?' she asks The Landlady.

'Do you really want to dig it out?'

'I want to know what's buried in there!' says The Former Banker's Writer Wife. 'What do you think?' she asks The Common Unemployed Boyfriend.

'I'll go either way,' he says. 'But I won't do the work!'

'I'll do it!' says The Former Banker's Writer Wife.

'This is so funny!' says The Landlady.

'Yes!' says The Former Banker's Writer Wife.

'OK, I'll get a trowel,' says The Landlady and disappears towards the kitchen.

'She even has a trowel!' says The Former Banker's Writer Wife. 'What's a trowel?'

'A sort of spade,' says The Common Unemployed Boyfriend. 'A gardening thingy, to make holes.'

'I see… This is great!'

'This isn't right,' says The Boring Civil Servant.

'Darling: chill out,' says The Common Unemployed Boyfriend.

'Yes, it's not like Fonzie will come back from the afterlife to kill us all,' says The Former Banker's Writer Wife.

'I know, stupid! But it isn't nice. Somebody's buried Fonzie there. Someone cared about Fonzie. Just leave Fonzie alone!'

'You're such a bore,' says The Former Banker's Writer Wife.

'You're only fun when you're drunk,' The Boring Civil Servant replies.

'That's correct,' says The Former Banker.

'OK, darling, take it easy. We'll bury Fonzie back afterwards. She had a pet fish called Fonzie when she was a kid,' explains The Common Unemployed Boyfriend apologetically.

'Yes,' says The Boring Civil Servant and starts crying. She leaves.

'Shit,' says The Former Banker.

'I didn't know…' says The Former Banker's Writer Wife.

'Oh, fuck it. She'll be fine. HAVE A DRINK DARLING,' shouts The Common Unemployed Boyfriend. 'Oh, look at him,' he points in my direction. 'What's up buddy!' But I miss all this. I never hear anything at all, because I'm knocked out.

'He's sleeping,' says The Former Banker.

'I'd forgotten about him with all this excitement,' says The Former Banker's Writer Wife. 'Remind me to get him a copy of my chapbook,' she says to her husband.

'I will.'

'What chapbook?' asks The Common Unemployed Boyfriend.

'Oh, don't worry,' says The Former Banker's Writer Wife. 'I think she likes him,' she says whispering.

'You THINK?' asks The Former Banker.

'Yeah, it's pretty obvious,' says The Common Unemployed Boyfriend.

'Don't be mean, guys,' says The Former Banker's Writer Wife.

'Anyway…' says The Common Unemployed Boyfriend and he pulls a face.

'What?' asks The Former Banker.

'Nothing…' says The Common Unemployed Boyfriend.

'Oh, come on!' says The Former Banker Writer's Wife.

'Nice lad…' says The Common Unemployed Boyfriend.

'Say it!' says The Former Banker's Writer Wife.

'Nothing!' says The Common Unemployed Boyfriend. 'Nice lad: that's it…'

They laugh — they understand. The Landlady comes back running.

'Here's the trowel. Now: DO IT!' she says giving the tool to The Common Unemployed Boyfriend.

'I said I wouldn't do the work…'

'Please: my back is hurting,' says The Former Banker's Writer Wife.

'Yes, please,' says The Former Banker.

'Come on! I'll get you a beer and massage your shoulders,' says The Landlady.

'OK! I'll do it,' he says.

'I love you, fatso,' says The Landlady and blows a kiss in his direction.

'I love you too,' says The Common Unemployed Boyfriend and moves towards the tombstone. He kneels before it and crosses himself.

'Be careful,' says The Former Banker's Writer Wife. 'I mean: be gentle. We don't want to destroy the corpse.'

'I will.'

They all gather around the kneeling man. The Common Unemployed Boyfriend sticks the trowel into the earth and shovels for the first time — the typical shovelling sound but in trowel scale: thinner.

'Spooky,' says The Former Banker.

'Ha,' says The Landlady.

'Shhhh, dears,' says The Former Banker's Writer Wife.

'Yeah guys, shut your mouth,' says The Common Unemployed Boyfriend.

He digs, shovelling carefully and piling up the earth on one side. A hole the size of a football suddenly materialises just before the tombstone. Everyone is silent and expectant except me. One shovel after another and soon he has dug about ten inches.

'It's buried quite deep,' says The Common Unemployed Boyfriend, all covered in dirt.

'Keep digging,' orders The Former Banker's Writer Wife.

'Go deeper,' says The Landlady.

'Do it,' says The Former Banker.

'OK,' he says and he keeps digging, deeper and deeper. The mound on the side grows. When he has dug an arm's length deep he stops.

'There's nothing in here, guys. I give up,' he says.

'What do you mean you "give up"?' asks The Former Banker's Writer Wife.

'Exactly that: I give up.'

'Don't spoil the party…' says The Former Banker.

'Dig it yourself, mate!'

'Do you think I can't do it?'

'I don't care, mate. It was your missus' idea. Dig it yourself,' he says and breaks off and disappears towards the kitchen.

'I think he's cross,' says The Landlady.

'He's just lazy,' says The Former Banker's Writer Wife. 'Why don't we wake him up and get him to finish the hole?' she asks the other two, pointing at me.

'He's too drunk,' says The Landlady. 'Let him sober up.'

'Is he THAT drunk?'

'Either that or he's very tired. He's been off for an hour. And he's snoring,' says The Former Banker.

'Would you finish digging then?' she asks her husband.

'It's quite deep already. I think we should call it off,' says The Former Banker.

'Damn you guys! You're so fucking useless,' his wife says. 'I'll dig it myself!' The Landlady follows the conversation with interest and a broad smile on her face.

'Wait!' says The Former Banker. 'Have you got a proper shovel? And a torch?' he asks.

'I've got a folding shovel. Not sure about the torch,' says The Landlady.

'I didn't know you were so much into gardening,' says The Former Banker's Writer Wife.

'Get it. And get some matches and some old newspapers,' he says.

'Right,' The Landlady says and runs back into the kitchen.

'I'm sorry that I called you useless,' says The Former Banker's Writer Wife.

'It's OK,' he says sulking.

'I mean it: I'm sorry,' she says. 'But I really want to see Fonzie...'

'It's fine, honey.'

'And I'm a bit drunk too...'

He doesn't reply. The Landlady comes back.

'Hey! I found a torch! I've brought newspapers and matches just in case.'

'Great,' says The Former Banker's Writer Wife.

'Let me see the torch,' says The Former Banker. He inspects it with care, from every side. Then he presses a button and the torch flashes with a strong light. He accidentally points it at me but I'm unbothered. 'Nice,' he says. 'OK... I need one of you to hold the torch behind me while I dig.'

'I can do that,' says The Landlady.

'Great.'

'Anything else?' asks his wife.

'For the moment that's all. Get me that shovel and let's get going. I don't want to miss *Match of the Day*.' He unfolds the shovel and then kneels before the hole dug by The Common Unemployed Boyfriend. The Landlady gets behind him and points with the torch while his wife watches from the side. He starts digging, shovelling, with might and intent, piling the earth on the side, one movement after the other, getting deeper into the ground. Soon the hole is over twenty inches deep. 'This shit is buried deep, for real,' he says.

'Don't give up, darling,' says his wife.

Digging.

Digging.

Digging.

Thirty, thirty-five, forty, forty-five. Fifty inches. The shovel is getting too short and he's almost falling into the hole.

Digging. Digging. And a knock.

'Gotcha!' he says.

'What is it? WHAT IS IT?'

'I can't see anything,' says The Landlady.

'Pass me the torch,' he says. He points the torch down. 'It looks like a wooden box.'

'A mini-coffin!' shouts The Landlady.

'Get it out!' says The Former Banker's Writer Wife.

He leans into the hole and gets his whole torso in to dig around the box.

'You'll put this in the wash when we get home,' he tells his wife.

'I always do it anyway!' she replies.

'Don't fight, dears,' says The Landlady.

Knock, knock.

He struggles for a while. Then he throws the shovel out of the hole and leans deeper. He pulls a muddied wooden box out and lays it on the ground. 'YES!' says his wife. The three of them stare in silence.

'Hmmm,' says The Former Banker.

'How do we open it?' asks The Landlady.

'Let me see,' he says.

'Come on! Come on! Open it!'

'It looks solid.'

'What do you mean solid?'

'Yeah, solid. It looks like oak and it's nailed. Or even welded… I can't see any joints… I don't think it's meant to be opened.'

'Break it with the shovel!' says his wife.

'It's Fonzie's coffin!' he says.

'Fuck Fonzie. We can bury him in a shoebox. Have you got a shoebox?' she asks The Landlady.

'Yes.'

'Do it.'

'OK,' he says. He hits the box with the shovel. The box is sturdy and doesn't give in. He bangs the box harder. Harder. Harder. Harder. Harder. I wake up and look around and see a huge hole, a big pile of dirt, a shovel, a torch and people looking at a wooden box. I think for a couple of seconds that they will bury me alive. Then I nod off again. 'I can't break it,' says the Former Banker.

'Can't you bang it harder?' asks his wife.

'The shovel is too light. I can't break it. Have you got a saw?'

'Nope,' says the landlady.

'I can't believe it…' says The Former Banker's Writer Wife.

'A hammer?'

'Yes, I've got a hammer,' she says and runs back to the kitchen.

She comes back with a hammer. The Former Banker starts banging on the box.

Hammering.

Hammering.

Hammering.

'It's not fucking giving!' says The Former Banker.

'Oh god! You are such a pansy!'

'Shut up! Try cranking this open yourself with these shit tools!'

'They're from Argos,' says The Landlady apologetically.

'Don't worry, dear. It's not the tools: it's him. He's a big fucking pansy.'

'Try yourself…' says The Former Banker, extending the hammer to his wife.

'That's a man's job. I'm not even going to hold that hammer…'

'God! I wish I hadn't married an alcoholic!' he says looking up to the night sky.

'He's going all melodramatic now!' says his wife. The Landlady follows the situation, once more with bemusement.

'Well… If you won't try yourself then that's it! I'm going home. Bye dear, sorry my wife is a cunt,' he says, turns and walks away.

'Bye…' says The Landlady.

'Can you believe this? Can you believe the shit I have to put up with? Can you?'

'Take it easy…'

'No, really… This is the last nail in the coffin, ironically… He's fucking useless. A failure. I wish I had married the other one.'

'Which other one?'

'Come on! The other one! You remember the other one! Don't you?'

'The Ginger Accountant?'

'Yes, The Ginger Accountant!'

'I thought he had ginger pubes and bad breath.'

'Yes, he did. But you can get used to that. What you can never get used to is living with a big, fat, useless, fucking pansy.'

'He grilled the sausages…'

'Even a kid can do that!'

'Yeah, that's true.'

'Shall we wakey-wakey him? I mean… he might be able to open it…' says The Former Banker's Writer Wife, of course talking about me.

'Let him sleep. He's too drunk. Shall I try myself?'

'No way, dear! You know what? Forget about it. Fuck Fonzie!' she says and kicks the box back inside the hole. 'Sorry we messed up your garden, dear.'

'Don't worry! It was fun!'

'Yeah it was, wasn't it? God, I don't want to go home now… Don't want to see that pathetic manchild for the rest of today…'

'Shall we finish the wine then?'

'Sure! Let's do that.'

'Let's go inside.'

'OK.'

The Landlady glances towards me.

'What shall we do with him?' she asks.

'Oh, leave him here! It'll help him sober up,' The Former Banker's Writer Wife says, while both of them walk up the stairs towards the kitchen.

'It's a bit cold out there…' The Landlady says and closes the kitchen door.

'Don't worry! Have you got cards?' She sits on a chair.

'I think so… Let me get the wine first…'

'Great! Fancy playing some poker?'

'I don't know how.'

'I'll teach you!'

'Fab!'

'Shall we play for money?'

'Teach me first!'

'You're right. By the way…' she takes her hand to her temple.

'What?'

'I almost forgot my chapbook!'

'Oh, yes!'

'Got fifteen pounds? You can ask him for the money when he wakes up.'

'Sure.'

The night sets in over Victoria Park Village. Swine-flavoured darkness, little gardens, thin gardens, claustrophobic gardens in narrow yet expensive houses, of constantly swelling prices, regardless of the crisis, the exoduses (different exoduses), this insular piece of dirt lost in the sea sinking, sinking, sinking into the North Atlantic, the North Sea. Sinking with all of us.

Still smoking — sometimes even burning — barbecues miles around. Disintegrating charcoal and cigarette butts, used matches and even chewing gum. Shrunk dehydrated sausages resting over rusty rails covered in pork fat and red peppers burnt to black, one per grill. Once or twice per half-mile a stray burger reduced to the size of a two-pound coin. Grilling paraphernalia turned dark with fire, fat, rust and general lack of use. Cancerous firestarters and half-full bags of damp carbon stones. Dismembered copies of broadsheets next to the barbecue — the World section burns faster, the Culture section burns last, celebrities' faces resist burning until botox heats up and it melts from the paper to the meat, 'Article 50' and 'financial markets' and 'pensions' and 'expats' and 'Brexit' written on half-burned pages. Empty bottles and cans. Half-full glasses, broken glasses, glasses with strange mixes — beer and rosé, beer and cigarette butts, wine and water, beer and Coke, beer and some strange unidentifiable green matter, vomit, the vomit of someone who had one fruit salad too many, spunk maybe, and dessert wine. Wayfarers left in remote corners. Forgotten keys, forgotten fags, forgotten iPhones, smartphones, Blackberrys, lesser Androids, bluetooth speakers, different Siris shouting into the void, speaking to other Siris, orphaned Siris. And forgotten watches, wallets, tobacco bags, spliffs, digital cameras (simil Leica, expensive), three-wheeler baby buggies, babies, condoms and inebriated adult guests.

Next to the grill.

'Let's go inside,' she says.

'What do you mean they're all gone?' I ask.

'Yes, they've been gone for hours,' says The Landlady.

'I swear they were all here, just a minute ago…'

'I think you've had too much to drink. You must have dreamt it. You were dead to the world, dear.'

'How embarrassing!'

'Oh, don't worry! You're just drunk!'

'You won't invite me anymore.'

'Come on! You just fell asleep! Let's go inside — I'm really cold and it looks like it'll rain. I'll get you a coffee.'

'What time is it?'

'Almost midnight.'

'Fuck.'

'Do you have to go?'

'No. But it's late.'

'Yes… Let's go.'

She helps me up and we walk into the kitchen. When we get to the kitchen I lean against the sink, open the tap and drink some water with my hands.

'I feel like shit,' I say.

'You drank too much, too soon,' she says and passes me an empty glass.

'You too!' I say shutting the tap off.

'But I don't feel like shit. Look: I'm ready to start partying again.' Her hair is a bit messed up, she's got mud on her dress and her eyes are a bit disoriented, but yes: she could probably start partying again. 'Shall I make you a coffee? It'll make you feel better.'

'Yes, please.'

'Have a seat.'

I sit by the table and watch her move around the kitchen. I try to follow her arse but my head is spinning.

'I'm sorry I got drunk like this,' I say.

'Oh, stop it! Really…' she replies without turning back from the kettle. 'You'll get better and better. You'll master it. How long you've been here?'

'Where? In London?'

'Yep.'

'Fifteen years… Something like that.'

'You should be trained by now…'

'I think it was the weed…'

'That's true. You need to avoid mixing. Not good at all. Rule number one: don't mix.'

'Yeah.'

'I mean it! Avoid at all costs! One thing at a time.'

'OK… Anyway… Have you got a taxi number I can call? Actually, I'll call myself an Uber.'

'Do you want to leave?'

'Not now, later.'

'You can stay here if you want — there's a sofa bed.'

'Really? Wouldn't you mind?'

'Not at all. You already pay for my other mortgage. It's the least I can do.'

She gives me the cup of coffee and sits next to me.

'I think I'll take tomorrow off,' I say.

'I was thinking the same,' she says.

'Are you feeling unwell too?'

'Not really. But I have to fix that mess in the garden.'

'What mess?'

'Don't you remember?'

'No… Do I have to remember? Was it me?' I ask concerned.

'No! It was us… It was fun! I'll show you tomorrow morning,' she says.

'Great. I don't want to get evicted,' I say. She laughs. 'Good coffee.'

'Thanks.'

'You're welcome.'

Silence.

'I liked your friends…'

'They liked you too.'

'Excellent!'

I blow into the mug and look inside: the black coffee, some bubbles moving in a centrifugal motion — it makes me feel sick. I look at her and she smiles. She sits next to me, stares at me.

'She left you a copy of her chapbook.'

'That's nice!'

'It's fifteen pounds. You can give it to me later. Or just add it to your rent.'

'Thanks.' I have a drink, blow into the mug, and drink again.

'Do you really like my coffee?'

'Yes! It's a great cup of coffee.'

'My tea is even better.'

'I don't have a single doubt,' I say. 'Your tea must be amazing.'

CEcI N'EsT PAS UN MéMOIRE

'During the next hour, everything you'll hear from us is really true and based on solid facts.'
ORSON WELLES, *F FOR FAKE*

A quick montage of family farewell, security checks, extortionate duty-free shops, boarding queues, the Overhead Compartment Wars, a safety announcement delivered by zombified attendants, eyes that reach for the nearest emergency exit, seat belts fastening, brain relocating to the stomach while the plane shoots away from the tarmac, pills gulped during a bout of turbulence over Uruguay, nodding off before the continent becomes a memory, and then — thousands of kilometres and several delirious dreams later — a stopover in Milan Malpensa.

Here, in a smoking area that I reach by inertia, I get rid of the cigarettes and the Argentine coins, in an overcooked attempt to reset, to start from scratch, to shed some existential kilos, to offload the detritus of a past self into an ashtray, sitting next to a broken man with yellow fingertips.

So first a fast succession of events and then this flow slowing down — time recovering its habitual shape during the past months: a time of waiting. Seven hours now. Then there will be an Aer Lingus flight to Dublin.

After which there will be one more of these places that look like shopping malls, with people pulling suitcases around, pushing trolleys, scrambling for the nearest exit, stinking of armpit sweat, bad breath, booze, the stench of airplane travel. There, stinking as well and still a bit zoned-out, I will wait for Fred, who's no longer Federico, and who's been living this side of the Atlantic since 1998. He will be late and I will have time to ponder over the meaning of the linoleum floors, the crushed cigarette butts, the luggage belts puttering in their oblong journeys a few metres past the gates to my left, the signage in English and Irish, the voices announcing things on the PA, and the change in accent in these voices — the first clues as to what these departures and arrivals entail. And Fred and I finally will be hugging each other after several years apart. Everything will be business as usual. Even with his paler complexion, his yellower teeth, his receding hair. And whatever he sees in me as a marker of the time we've lost.

But all this I don't know yet.

Now there's just the cigarettes and the coins in an ashtray in Milan Malpensa. The broken man and his yellow fingertips. The waiting. The future as the inconceivable mass that follows the waiting.

Smoke will get in my eyes in a parking lot, after Fred offers me one of his Marlboro Lights.

After a short ride on the airport shuttle, and after dropping my stuff in his room somewhere in the north of Dublin, we will stroll down O'Connell's Street. I won't pay much attention to anything in particular, trying to take everything in as a whole, barely registering Fred's glossolalic hum, failing to imprint memories beyond those coordinates provided by the nouns that will be resonating in my head: Ireland, Dublin, Fred, O'Connell's Street.

Everything will be a blur until we walk into an internet café and into different phone booths. Across the fake wooden wall full of Sharpie gibberish and telephone numbers scribbled next to pictures of hearts and names and ejaculating dicks, I will overhear Fred having a conversation in English. Yes, yes. No, no. Tomorrow, OK, sure, text me first thing in the morning if... yes, sure no problem... sure... of course... thanks... Then Fred will go quiet and I will be left on my own in my booth; I will try to call home. But I will forget to add the international code and will get nothing, followed by an angry tone. I will hang up, lift the receiver once more. I will key in 0054, repeating the numbers in my head to guide my fingers on the keypad, and finally I will hear the usual minimalist melody when a telephone rings in an empty room on the other end of the line. Until a person in the no longer empty room will lift the receiver. And then there will be a conversation with my mother that I won't retain very well. Yet all conversations with mothers are more or less the same, so we can infer how the exchange will go: the interrogation regarding the quality of the flight; the excited comment about our apparent aural proximity; the curiosity over where I am, what part of the city; the invitation to look after myself. And a variation of the Conversation with a Mother theme: an unnecessarily dramatic and motherly 'I miss you' — Argentine telenovela words that I am not yet trained to reciprocate. And then, when the silence starts to feel too uncomfortable, my promise to call again soon.

As we leave I will tell Fred that I couldn't recall the international code. Fred will say weird isn't it and I will agree. And here there will be the realisation, the awareness of the change, of the cut. Like when someone dies or someone is born —realising that things are no longer the same, that they can't be the same.

Minutes later, after another brief walk during which I won't register anything trying to take in all at once, I will be sitting by the window in Fitzsimmon's, a hopelessly obvious pub in the hopelessly obvious Temple Bar, drinking Jameson's and Guinness, already quite dizzy and surrounded by Fred and some other nameless Argentines, watching tourists stroll down the road. By this point the feeling of self-strangeness triggered by the international code incident will a familiar acquaintance. This sensation that I'm always watching myself from somewhere else, or as if I was someone else.

Unable to yet do anything with this I will think OK, *this* is where I am *now*. *This* is where I am *now*, I will think, trying to find a solid point from which to start living this part of my life. *This* is where I am *now*, I will repeat mantra-like, as people in fluorescent windbreakers and trainers walk past, contorted by the weight of massive and unnecessary SLR cameras. And *this* is where I am *now*, I will think and repeat uncountable times since then, the *this* and the *now* jumping back and forth. Ungraspable *thises* and *nows*.

Then there will a smelly pub called the Welcome Inn. The nameless Argentines will have been left behind — most live south of the river, Fred will explain at some point in the night, connoting something I will miss. So there will be just Fred and I in this unremarkable hole, mixing what's left of my sleeping pills with pints of beer, battered by first- and second-hand smoking, surrounded by bloated fuchsia drunks.

Later there will be zigzagging all the way to Fred's house. There will be puking in a small waste bin in his room, sleeping with clothes on after collapsing on a thin mattress. And soon the light of day will barely pierce through the blinds but will still wake me up — my first night in Dublin followed by my first morning, the passage from one to the other impossible to discern, a terrible headache acquired in between.

This is Dublin, tomorrow. My tomorrow now but also Fred's tomorrow, the one he will have uttered in that internet café, in the yesterday of this first morning in Dublin. And his tomorrow will mean a sentence to full-time employment. More precisely a kitchen porter job in a canteen in an office building south of the river, where Fred has been working for a year and a half. It will take a few minutes for him to convey that he isn't joking, that in the Dublin of the Celtic Tiger a job can be found with just a phone call, and that he has found me one, and that we will need to walk thirty minutes, because apparently no one uses the bus here. No, no time for breakfast, not even for a cup of coffee, no time for a cigarette, just brush your teeth, man, mask that breath a bit, and off we go, you should be happy, working the day after you arrived. And soon we will be out in the drizzle.

There will be walking, Fred several metres ahead of me. There will be houses that all look the same and several novel shades of grey every way I look. The closed shop shutters will be different. The traffic signs will be different. There will be no electricity cables above. Even dereliction will be different. And soon there will be a bridge and a malnourished river — a sad stream of dark green water coming from who knows where, flowing towards the sea, meeting the sea in some place I won't be able to imagine. And there will be the need to compare size with that other river I have left behind, that I cursed for twenty-five years but that on this bridge will feel exuberant, majestic, an ocean of a river. And I will declare my disappointment at the way this city looks in the morning, so different from the sheep-blessed idyl in that Thomas Cook guide I picked up in a bookshop back home, that more or less decided the rest of my life. And Fred will say that I won't be happy anywhere and he might be right. Maybe I have always been unsettled, dissolved, the perfect sequel to people who lived and died looking back home. A mythical place that they would have hated, should planes have been invented fifty years earlier, had they been able to return, to let time and habit kill their homesick ideation. But they didn't return, so the nostalgia caught like a disease, became part of the family's DNA. Maybe I'm tracing those journeys in the negative, I will fantasise; maybe I'm going back to the start, to some kind of origin, in search of some kind of reparation. Because it will take some more immigration officers until I shake off the illusion that I belong this side of the ocean.

All this mental dialogue with dangerous existential overtones will be done crossing the Liffey in slow motion, while I get used to a present that entails crossing bridges on foot. While I stop for a second to spit and watch my spit reach the water after dancing briefly in the wind, and then stare at a shopping trolley, the soon-to-be-forgotten supermarket name still visible under the water. There will be a bicycle underwater too, more indiscernible trash that the river has failed to wash all the way down to the sea. And in my head there will be ruminations over the things people throw into rivers in different parts of the world, a moment of toying with Heraclitus. But there is nothing to be gained from these attempts at philosophy because it will be too early in the morning.

And soon this episode of river-watching will be left behind. Even if from this airport in Milan it is still the future and leaving the future behind is beyond the realms of possibility. Now there is just this café where they serve a decent espresso that I pay mentally for in Argentine currency, making it the most expensive coffee I have ever had. Now I am just a recent non-smoker with a flight to catch in four hours. Now I am still oblivious to the fact that tomorrow, soon after crossing the Liffey, after being gifted a pair of gloves, an apron, a silly-looking white hat, and an induction of five minutes — mostly health-and-safety truisms and a couple of basics on how to use the industrial dishwasher — I will spend most of the day working a metallic scrubber on a pot.

Some things — dishes, cutlery, glasses — will go in the dishwasher; the pans and pots must be tackled by hand. Two, three, a hundred times I will wash the same large pot before 10 a.m. and the pot will go two, three, a hundred times back to the chef, who will make it dirty again two, three, a hundred times, to then pass it back to me, and so on, in a culinary re-enactment of Sisyphus's plight. The dishes, cutlery, glasses, pans, pots, everything, will start pilling up because the dishwasher is too slow and why wash the same pot over and over if he'll make it dirty again?

A kitchen where you could use some help can be a lonely place and Fred will be at the carvery, getting everything ready for lunch, taking his time arranging the food in elaborate ways, not so much seized by an aesthetic impetus but to work as little as possible. Come on now, will ye clean up those fuckin dishes, we can't have them eating off fuckin trays, can we. Or something like that, accented, grammatically disconcerting, in a tongue that sounds close to English but that is nowhere near what my teacher Miss Oitaven sold me as English back in the mid 1980s. Nothing like *Sam on Radio 3, 2, 1*, *Sam on Channel 9*, or *Sam by Satellite*, the textbooks of those days, so British, so BBC, received pronunciation, every English speaker either a lady or a gentleman. Go on, will ye clean them things and I'll clean these other things and be done with it, fuck's sake, Simon the chef will shout once more, fuckin grabbing the thing from my hand and fuckin pushing me away from the sink while he assaults the thing with a scrub. And like this it will go on for a while, him scrubbing, me washing dishes by hand. Until the dishwasher's cycle ends and he goes back to the stove with his beloved pot.

Just a couple of days ago I was sitting in a bar, unhatted and unaproned, relaxed and carefree, I will think while I dry glasses with a long piece of blue kitchen roll. And to think that I fancied things would always be the same, wherever I went. True, the whole country was sinking in shit: everyone had left, was leaving, or was thinking of leaving, figuring out how to get their money out of the bank, if the bank still existed. True, everyone was talking about leaving or about those who had left, mostly to hide in Barcelona for a while, wait for the worst to pass, do the Grand Tour around the Old Continent, catch some imported STDs, gather nice memories. I wasn't averse to talking about leaving too, in the company of some of my friends who were still there, who will remain there forever because that's who they are and they can't fathom dying a kilometre away from the place where they were released into the void. But I monologued, blasé. I indeed delivered a departure speech, but as with an actor delivering a well-rehearsed soliloquy there was a whiff of fabulation to my words. In my mind it was more like a game than a leap into the unknown — an extended holiday without a clear itinerary — an adventure — the opening lines of a Bildungsroman with a happy ending.

Maybe deep inside I knew well I was fooling myself. But I didn't want to think too much about it, so first I'm going to Dublin and I'll get a good job, anything, I'm not fussy. Maybe as a tour guide, or in a museum, or as an interpreter, somewhere, anything along those lines — Fred can help me. Because they need people in the tourist industry, people who can speak English, yes, but also other languages, and no one asks many questions about your papers as long as you work hard. So just work, save money, and travel a bit around the country. Stay long enough to get my head around things abroad, get confident. Then move to London where you get a six-month tourist visa, use the work experience in Dublin to get an even better job, and when the visa expires join a cheap language college and stay longer, now as a student. And then just bide my time. Maybe even attend the course and get a Cambridge Proficiency certificate. Wait for the Italian papers to arrive; it's only a matter of time, as the guy in the Italian consulate said. Then perhaps move to Madrid, go back to university, get a philology or a comparative literature degree, something clever-sounding; anything to compensate for the past six years studying classical music in a conservatory full of idiots. One of them, Ángel — older than us, a retired lawyer — was quiet, smoking, observing my performance. Until he couldn't stay quiet any longer and said you should stay and brave the storm like we did;

instead you're running away to go and wait tables for the English. I laughed. I said that this boy wasn't going to wait any table, no way. They need intelligent people over there; they need eager, resourceful people like me. And I was going to Ireland, maybe I would go to London too, but the only thing I knew for sure was that I was going to Ireland, that the story would start there and who knows where things would take me. I couldn't stay in Argentina, couldn't take it any more, just couldn't keep looking for work in the paper every Monday morning, when everything available was selling mobile phones, commissions only, and you had to queue for four hours to end up working for peanuts. What kind of future can you build like this? If he had been twenty-five he would have done the same this time — if he was sincere he would agree. Because there was no epic quest in staying to sell mobile phones, and soon no one would give a fuck about mobile phones either. There was no great fight worth fighting for in 2001. No chance of playing Che Guevara like you and your delusional friends back in the '70s. Maybe my mistake had been not listening to my grandmother when she said I would starve as a musician and I should study something else, management, business administration, accountancy, IT, something short and useful. Maybe my mistake was committing to things one hundred per cent, all or nothing, take no prisoners. The past six years it had been music. And the time had come to leave and I was committing one hundred per cent to that, I said, telling myself that this commitment was bullshit, like all my other commitments, but by this time also quite certain that whatever would happen wasn't up to me to decide any more. But I didn't say this. I just said that somehow things would make sense, they always do, sooner or later. I would find a way. I'd have a brilliant idea at some point and I'd be saved. It was my fate to be saved. I'm like a cat, right? Somehow I'll fall on my feet. Ángel didn't reply; he just smoked, in silence.

Just a couple of days later I will be scrubbing the pan once more, after having finished the dishes and the glasses. I will have lost count of the precise numbers of times this will have happened. And I will pass the pot back to Simon.

And every day will blend into one. And the days will turn into weeks.

Up early in the morning with a terrible headache. Walk under the rain, Fred always a few metres ahead, taciturn, smoking. I will be following, trying to catch up, smoking too, cursing, still physically unprepared for all this bipedal moving across space. The grey houses. The closed shop shutters. The traffic signs. No electricity cables hanging above. Dereliction. And then the bridge, the trolley, the bike. Spitting at the Liffey with the rage of one who spits not at a river but at a country he can't understand yet, but already resents, because of a stupid sense of superiority, that some things are below me, that some people just shouldn't sell mobile phones let alone wash dishes for a living, even if they have to; all this paired with a very Argentine propensity for drama and tragedy, a tendency to think that things are the way they are and they can't ever change, that everything you do is ultimately a prison, in some way, and that I will die in front of the industrial dishwasher fifty years from now, with Simon passing me back the pot or asking me to fuckin pass it back to him will ye. And occasionally the thought of foetuses aborted and disposed of in the river, and the wish they were more, that everyone outside of the kitchen, in this cold bog of a city, threw themselves into the Liffey and drowned with a turd in their mouth, because they don't understand me — they can't see my true potential for something I don't yet know myself what it is but the potential is there; these bastards condemning me to the miserable life of a kitchen porter, instead of receiving me like a genius, just because I was born elsewhere and no one wants to wash dishes in their own country, not if they can do something else. Then calming down, walking a bit more, until we get to the building where we work. And one more cigarette before going in, sitting outside. And then the repetition of a relatively limited number of manoeuvres, executed over and over again, for eight hours, interrupted only for a twenty-minute lunch break, a couple of sneaky fags in the alley in the back, and the generally uneventful round to check the toilets.

The days in the kitchen will be punctuated by nights of drink. Friday night binges that extend into Sunday nights. Culturally-impaired bloated bladders being relieved against walls in dark alleys. Stumbling all the way to Fred's, getting lost, arriving somehow, getting lost again, arriving again, but arriving differently. And strange moods in which I will find myself, unaccustomed to so much booze, to the national lack of guilt around this carnivalesque self-destruction. And failed attempts at courting — fictitious telephone numbers being handed by also drunk but smarter locals. Confidence and self-esteem averaging negative numbers and Fred and I staggering horny and pissed all the way home, saying and doing things we will regret.

So there will be a heavier kind of silence on the way to work, the kitchen a momentary break, Fred leaving work early to see a man about a dog or the Irish equivalent, and me finding a room of my own, where the heating won't work, and I will never know the name or face of my housemates, if there is actually any other human being in the house. At least my move will bring some peace. And Fred and I will start speaking again, like an old spring returning to its usual form.

Then there will be more gallons of petroleum-coloured beer. More Argentines with irrelevant names, from whom I will run away in order to avoid acting the nostalgic Argentine abroad in the company of others acting their own nostalgic character. And short escapades in slow trains that will leave me in the middle of nowhere, in small stations I won't leave, where I will just cross to the other platform and ride the train back to Dublin. Walks in St Stephen's Green, Phoenix Park, the banks of the Liffey somewhere near the sea, an attempt to enjoy Belfast during a two-hour visit with Fred, and a place full of rocks on the west coast but that could be anywhere else in Ireland. Time that flies when you are either scrubbing a pot or drunk — a visa that nears its end. And then one night a party in Sandymouth, where I'll get seriously stoned and start thinking that I'm far away from everyone who knows me, and feel scared and exhilarated, free for the first time, alone yes, and about to become *illegal* too, but also divorced from everything and everyone that ever held me back — everything and everyone but Fred. And you can't start from zero unless you reach a proper blank page. One hundred per cents; all of nothings. I need to offload the existential weight that remains, get rid of the detritus and so on. While I get another stamp on my passport and avoid being sent back home.

After all of this has been consigned to the past, I may be sitting in a café in London. Seventeen years will have elapsed between Milan Malpensa, and the scooping out of sugar from the bottom of a sour espresso in a place with ironic posters of Bruce Springsteen and heavily tattooed people.

Maybe another Thomas Cook guide will have decided the next destination. I might have found it on a table at the Kylemore, or some pub. Or maybe it won't have been another Thomas Cook guide and the idea will have come into my head in a bookshop near Trinity College, when I accidentally bump into a Cortázar book. Or maybe it will have been a cheap flight announced in a travel agent's window, or an advert in a newspaper, someone wearing a beret, the perfume of hot bread and the thought of a baguette, a documentary about Jim Morrison's final days, overhearing someone say 'hors d'oeuvre', wondering what it means, what secrets these words conceal, going after these words, or the promise of relaxed passport controls. Somehow the choice will have been Paris, in a couple of weeks from that night in Sandymouth, in just under three months from now.

And then a taciturn trip with Fred to the same airport that is about to welcome me in a while. A quick farewell but really a goodbye, that I will have made sure is quick and clinical by rushing through security after some poor excuse about planes, anxiety, toilets. Then there will have been an uneventful flight. Another arrival at one of those places that look like a shopping mall. A bus ride to a station, some station. An extortionate taxi ride to a hostel someone — who? — will have booked for me. Then some months in Paris, the clichéd birth of writing in a picturesque café. Yes, the Birth of Writing. The handling of pens, notebooks, pointless notes towards pointless books, some that will be written, some that won't.

And after this all my life will have tuned into an amorphous mass. Hostages of the narcissism of first person narration, the I who writes, and the written I, will have mixed to the point of unrecognition. So I may be sitting in a café in London reading these words. And I may be trying to figure out what is actually real, and what made-up. Or I might well be rejoicing in the uncertainty. Or aware of the fantasy, I might be rejoicing in the fabrication. Or maybe I will read these four thousand or so words, one more time, as I correct the punctuation here and there, and find that everything written here is my life, verbatim. That regardless of how much I have tried to hide I have failed, and I am naked on the page.

But all this I don't know yet.

And if I did know, would it even matter?

THE KID AND THE TELEPHONE BOX

The sign said Rome and pointed to the left but we pressed right ahead. It was an average circular road with scattered flat houses, advertisement boards, cars rushing in this or that direction, smog, vast expanses of industrial space, empty soft drink cans and rubbish lying on the hard shoulder. Manuel was driving, I was sitting next to him, and Mika was in the back, filming everything with a small camcorder.

'Why didn't you turn left?' I asked.

'Sorry?'

'There was a sign for Rome. I thought we were going to Rome.'

'You take it easy and let me do the driving. Just relax.'

Relax… Everybody says that all roads lead to Rome but apparently this is a myth — at least in its periphery. And to make matters worse all circular roads look the same. We could have been driving near Rosario, São Paulo, London, Paris, Kathmandu, Leeds, Johannesburg, Mexico DF, San Francisco, Ontario, Reykjavik, anywhere or almost anywhere.

Manuel took a right turn and we went over a level crossing. The car slowed down and this guy who was standing by the barrier looked into my eyes, I don't know why. Soon we took a narrow street uphill. Manuel drove fast and the cars driving towards us drove fast too. Once or twice in the space of a hundred metres we narrowly avoided a crash, but everything seemed calculated, precise — there was a prearranged agreement. Mika was quiet, her mind focused on her camera and the camera was focused on me. Or maybe she was just filming the passing cars. I didn't turn around to find out.

'We're not going to Rome,' Manuel said.

'Cool,' I said. He was waiting for me to ask where we were going. It felt right to keep him waiting.

And more narrow roads, more steep roads, the smell of pine trees. Manuel would occasionally point to this or that place. He wouldn't give any explanation, just point to this or that place and tell me to look at something.

Look there, a typical Italian house.

Look there, a church.

Look there, a path getting lost somewhere.

A pig.

A mountain.

Greenish fields.

Vineyards.

A convent.

A dog.

More vineyards, another vineyard, another convent.

That's not a pig, it's a Great Dane.

And so on.

Twenty minutes later we reached a town called Rocca di Papa. Manuel parked the car by a little square.

'Fancy a walk?'

'Sure,' I said.

It must have been three o'clock in the afternoon, the streets were empty and the sun was already weak. We left the car and crossed to the other side of the road, where there was a viewpoint on top of a steep cliff. Manuel leaned against the railing and lit up a cigarette; he passed me the pack and I lit up too. Mika was pointing the camcorder at me and I looked down below and saw a dog scavenging food from a bin bag. It was full of rubbish down there, in what looked like someone's back garden. How irritating it must be, to have everyone in town and every visitor dumping their shit into your backyard. I turned around to look at Mika and instead of seeing Mika I saw a camera lens. She gestured from behind the lens — I passed the cigarettes her way; Manuel elbowed me.

'Look,' he said. 'Over there, that's where Rome is. Happy now?' I looked towards the horizon: a palette of yellows and light greens and grey clouds coming from what looked like small garden bonfires.

'I can't see anything, only smoke,' I said.

'Can you repeat that again? I forgot to press REC,' Mika said. She nodded and smiled.

'I can't see anything, only smoke,' I repeated. She gave me the thumbs up.

'Behind the smoke is Rome,' Manuel said.

Mika had been with the camera in my face since I had

arrived the day before. Cameras feel like guns sometimes and it's impossible to get used to them and everybody hates a close-up. But I didn't complain, it's the direction things are going right now, no point in fighting that. We are constantly observed, photographed, filmed — Warhol's 'fifteen minutes of fame' dictum taken to its logical conclusion: we'll all have our fifteen minutes of registered irrelevance on a daily basis. When Mika finished her cigarette she tossed it down the rock face and filmed it; I looked at the cigarette all the way to the bottom and so did Manuel. The cigarette fell on the rubbish but missed the dog.

Soon we started walking again, sloping upward a narrow street that seemed to get narrower with every step. The sun, barely visible, dropped between tall houses, breaking through clothes hanging out to dry from side to side. My eyes hurt from the sun even though it was almost gone. The scene was too picturesque to be taken seriously, too typically Italian, in a way I couldn't really explain although I'm half Italian, or so says my passport.

'Tomorrow we can go to Rome... if you want,' he said. I didn't reply but I thought that I would just take the train to Rome and fuck him and his car — he was in control of the situation as long as he could drive me around. I was going to go to Rome on my own. Or maybe just stay in bed all day. Or maybe just take the plane back to London and spend Christmas on my own, waiting for Sabina to change her mind. I didn't know. Mika, who was lagging a few metres behind, turned back to the little square we had just left, filming, of course; Manuel caught me staring at her.

'I bought the camera for her birthday,' he said. 'She wants to do films.'

'Nice camera.'

'It would be good if you talked to her about it, give her a few tips. You know the drill.'

'Not really.'

'I thought you worked with films…'

'I do. I did. But I don't do films.'

'I thought you wrote a couple of scripts or things like that?'

'Yes, sort of.'

'So?'

'Writing is different. But I could never do a film. I wouldn't know where to start.'

'Still. Talk to her about films when you have a chance. Give her a list of films to see, a book to read, something. She's a nice girl. A bit slow, but good with visual things. She's obsessed with that fucking camera. She says she wants to do a documentary, but she doesn't have a clue.'

'That's commendable,' I said. 'I mean, documentaries are great.'

'Yeah, whatever; it keeps her busy. Talk to her. I hate documentaries…'

'Manu, can I have your shades, please?'

'No way!' he said. 'It's not even sunny!'

'I didn't sleep last night and I've got this terrible hangover. Lend me the shades, will you?'

He passed me a pair of aviators; I put them on. The sky was nicer staring from behind them; the sky is always nicer from behind a pair of sunglasses.

We continued walking and soon we reached what looked like the town centre. The streets were empty and all the shops were closed — it was dead quiet.

'Take me to a bar, Manu. This is depressing,' I said.

'Have you seen any bars?'

'There MUST be a bar…'

'Don't bet on it.'

He was right, maybe there wasn't a bar. The only visible thing was the end of the hill and a group of teenage girls coming our way. Manuel stared at them as they walked past. He turned around and saw that Mika was quite far, filming something high above, probably the clouds.

'They wear too much make-up but I'd do them anyway.'

'They are too young.'

'You think too much…' I knew he would say that. I didn't reply.

We reached the top of the hill — there was a church. All of the town was standing there, on the sidewalk, in the middle of the square. Cars parked everywhere. The old and the young, kids running around. A funeral, a wedding, a baptism, something, a reason to put make-up on, to wear your good clothes, to turn up in a shiny car. We walked past a group of teenage boys — I found it striking that several of them had plucked eyebrows. It must have been a fad.

'Salve,' said Manuel . 'C'è un bar qui intorno?'

He spoke with them for a while, then said grazie a couple of times and we kept walking.

'There's a café up there,' he said. Mika caught up with us.

'I shouldn't be filming you from behind,' she told Manuel. 'You're going bald.' Manuel didn't answer. She stopped filming him and directed the camera towards me. I threw my cigarette on the floor and tried to crush it with my left foot but missed it, stumbled, and kept walking to break a fall.

'You missed the cigarette butt. Why?' asked Mika.

'What do you mean "why"?'

'Yes. Did you miss it on purpose?'

'Not really. I should have tried with my right foot,' I said.

'Do you want to do another take?' she asked.

'Sure.' We went back some metres and she filmed me trampling on the butt. Manuel watched from the distance. I found the second take easier than the first one.

'Cut,' said Mika and we kept walking.

At some point, we reached a little square with a fountain, a telephone box, a café, and a couple of tables by the sidewalk. Manuel walked into the café; Mika and I sat at one of the little tables. It crossed my mind that Manuel hadn't asked what we wanted to have. He would probably bring a coffee when all I wanted was a large glass of red wine.

'He didn't ask...' I said.

'He never asks,' said Mika from behind the camera. She was filming the centrepiece, some floral tacky thing. I looked around — there was a fat kid playing with the telephone box, shoving a piece of wire manically into the coin slot. I became hypnotised with him, jerking the wire, completely taken over by his piece of wire and the phone box, on and on and on, making love to it. God knows what he was trying to achieve or if he could even think of achieving anything. He was one with that wire and the phone box. I envied him.

'Film that retard,' I said to Mika and she pointed the camera towards him and eyed me from behind the lens — she didn't say anything but I felt her disapproval. 'Yes,

I shouldn't use that word,' I said and winked at her. She smiled back and then kept filming the kid.

'Fuck!' she said.

'What?'

'I've run out of batteries!' She laughed very loud; I laughed too.

'Just look at him instead. Then film yourself talking about him, at home. Film yourself talking about not being able to capture what you see, something like that,' I said. 'It would work well. It's self-reflexive and people like self-reflexive things.'

'What do you mean by "self-reflexive"?' she asked.

'As in a film about making a film,' I said.

'That's brilliant,' she said and lit up a new cigarette. She stayed quiet, watching the kid. 'You know a lot about film,' she added a bit later.

'Yes,' I said.

'Give me a tip.'

'Oh, that's hard.'

'Just one tip,' she said.

'You mean another one!'

'Come on!'

'It's all in the details.'

'Interesting… How?'

'Yes… In the details, like that kid and the phone booth. If this was a film about me… Let's say it's a film about me going through some unspeakable shit: I'd pay more attention to details like that kid and the telephone box instead of paying much attention to me.'

'What does he have to do with you?'

'Nothing!'

'Nothing?'

'Exactly! It's in the details, the mood.'

She stayed quiet.

'I'll think about it,' she said at last, and smiled, just as Manuel came back and placed a tray with three espressos on our table.

We stayed a bit longer, Manuel and I chatting about Christmas, about never going back home this time of the year, about how we'd rather not go back at all, about how it's impossible after a while, how it doesn't make any sense. Mika stayed quiet throughout, listening, smiling at me tenderly every now and then, taking in the details, I guess, thinking about her film about a film.

When we left, the kid was still there, shoving his piece of wire into the phone box in the dark.

SOMETHING ABOUT THIS SUMMER AND THE SUMMER LAST YEAR

To Beatriz Viterbo

The house sits on top of a hill.

It must be ten thirty in the evening and we're still playing tennis on the clay court. We've been playing for a while, but after I throw a volley Nico connects a smash and the ball — our last one — disappears over the hedge, downhill, where it'll be swallowed by the sea overnight, like all the other balls. This means I've won. But Nico doesn't agree and throws the racquet in my direction, missing me by an inch or two. We insult each other, barely kept apart by the net, until he calls me a 'big-eared poof' and I run back inside.

In the lounge Patricio and Seba watch music videos and drink Coke straight from a glass bottle. I sit in the armchair behind the sofa, worried that they'll torture me as they've been doing for the past two weeks, pulling my ears and sideburns, beating me up, or pinning me to the ground to play yo-yo with spit on my face. But both are hypnotised by the screen.

A tall man wearing a hat walks through some catacombs carrying a blonde woman, probably dead.

There are candles everywhere. The tall man repeats the same lines over and over and I ask what he's singing. Seba replies that it's 'something about this guy called Jimmy' and Patricio laughs, they both laugh; I laugh too but I don't get the joke. The music video ends with the tall guy twitching in a white room with padded walls while the blonde woman, now alive and dressed in beige with a sweater wrapped around her neck, teases him. Now that the music is over I know I'll get it. But suddenly we hear Nico scream and we run outside to rescue him from under one of those things they use to flatten the tennis court.

The cast runs from ankle to knee. Nico tried to pull the court roller downhill and got his leg crushed against a rock. His ankle is broken but Carlos and Alicia decide we won't cut the holiday short — 'it won't change anything,' they said, and 'it's only a small fracture'. They're right, it won't change anything for them. Because now Nico won't be able to get in the water and he'll expect me to skip the water too. I'm supposed to keep him company, just like Seba is supposed to keep Patricio company. This is why they invited us here. That's what Alicia told my mother. It might be something to do with Helga.

We wake up late and Carlos grills a large piece of flank steak, sausages, sweetbread and black pudding. We drink three bottles of Coke and Carlos and Alicia drink two and a half bottles of wine — the barbecue is too salty, we all agree. After eating Patricio and Seba say they'll go downtown, Carlos and Alicia stumble upstairs to take a nap and Nico and I stay downstairs watching the telly.

A short brown alien with big blue eyes rummages through the trash.

It's the third time we've watched the film while we've been here. We now know the dialogue by heart and laugh a lot at the 'E.T. home phone' part, which Nico repeats with a metallic voice and a cushion cover for a hat. And then we catch an old Argentine comedy about a guy who doesn't want to go to work and stays in bed all day, lazying around and calling his wife names.

A man pinches his wife's bottom as she walks past.

We watch the film all the way through because of the tits. But this film must be an exception because there are no tits. And Argentine films, when they don't have tits, apart from an exception, are a waste of time.

When the cicadas go quieter we go down to the dunes round the back of the house. The sun is weaker now but there's no wind and the air is full of bugs and so thick you could slap it. Nico has trouble walking and he moans each time he pulls his right leg from the sand. He complains that it itches, and says that the ankle isn't really broken, that it's all a plot by his parents to ruin his summer. I tease him saying that it is broken for real, that he might get gangrene, and that they'll have to chop it off, that it'll be really bad but that he'll save a lot of money on shoes — he doesn't find it funny. Finally, he limps all the way to the trees, and we sit there, in the shade, cursing, spitting and throwing pinecones at each other.

When we get bored of this too, we build a small castle with twigs and leaves. We're about to build a second one so that we can have a war when Patricio and Seba turn up, kick the castle to the ground, pull my ears and tell us to fuck off back to the house. Nico says that he'll tell Alicia about their escapes to the dunes and the smoking. Patricio threatens us with telling Carlos about the money that vanished from the kitchen. We leave before things escalate and go back inside.

Some guys with weird hair and make-up sing a strange song in a strange greenhouse; there are caterpillars on the piano keyboard and the keys move up and down as if they had springs underneath.

Four men dressed in camouflage dance with an oil rig in the background.

A blond skinny guy with bad teeth plays an electric guitar on top of a mountain; he's wearing white gloves.

Patricio and Seba come back from the dunes and beat the living shit out of us while a brunette woman crosses a bridge, drives a car, rides on a horse, all in the space of three or four minutes, the time it takes for our living shit to get beaten.

Then we spend the rest of the night hunting for caterpillars but catching fireflies instead, watching them switch off one by one.

A picture of Helga on the mantelpiece. She's dressed in her First Communion clothes, her hands united in prayer, smiling at the camera. It looks like a professional photo and it must have been taken not long before the day she tried to rewind a cassette without leaving the swimming pool. She looks nothing like Nico and Patricio; she looks like a nice person, a bit like Alicia. Big brown eyes and brunette hair; pale face and delicate hands. I never met her, I was never invited back then. I wish I had met her at least once.

Helga's room in this house remains locked and nobody talks about her. But she's everywhere and there are still traces of her all around. Drawings, her face in a large and yellowing family photo hanging from the kitchen wall, books, magnets on the fridge, a pink bike, her parents' naps and empty bottles of wine. A Hello Kitty eraser forgotten under a cushion.

I kept it in my pocket and every now and then I smell it. In my mind Helga smells of strawberries but I've heard the dead smell of rotten flowers and naphthalene.

Carlos and Alicia say that we're going to another beach, that we need to go somewhere with a tent, because of Nico and his broken ankle. Patricio and Seba say they'll stay. Nico pretends to light a cigarette, releasing the smoke into the air, but his parents don't see him. Patricio licks his right index and shoves it in Nico's ear. Carlos and Alicia miss this too.

We drive downtown. It takes us half an hour to find a parking space near the casino and at least fifteen minutes of walking under the sun to reach the beach. There's hardly any space left in the sand — it's all cluttered with parasols and mats and people in colourful bathing suits; the air smells of tanning lotion, cigarettes, car fumes and mortadella sandwiches. The engines from the neighbouring avenue, brought by the wind, mask the sound of the sea, which is nowhere to be seen because the beach has a slope in the middle.

We've got one of the tents at the back, a large green thing with a pitched canvas roof. There must be a thousand identical tents stretching until the eyes can no longer see. It took us at least ten more minutes of Nico's moaning to find the right number. Now Carlos and Alicia are sleeping on the loungers, snoring, and Nico is reading Alicia's fashion magazine. Every now and then he rips a page out, folds it into a square, and then puts the piece of paper away in his pocket. I can't figure out why.

We play a game of cards and Nico wins. He taunts me while I ignore him and play a game of Solitaire. Carlos and Alicia wake up at one point and go back to sleep pretty quickly, after having a couple of swigs from the bottle of red they've been keeping from the heat in a portable cooler. When Nico falls asleep too, with the magazine on his face, I escape.

I run, free and wild, like the boy in this black and white film they showed the other night on the telly and that everyone but Carlos hated. I can't remember what the film was about but just before the end the boy was running on an empty beach, running away from something or someone, just like me now, and then it said 'FIN' over his body and I couldn't find out if he managed to escape or not. But here the beach is packed and it takes me at least five minutes to get to the water, jumping over stretched and crumpled towels, zig-zagging with burning feet around parasols and sunbathers.

I finally make it to the shore. The sea is dark and dirty and there's all sorts of trash floating in it: white plastic glasses, nylon bags, paper, cigarette butts, seaweed, pieces of wood, fish scales, and what looks like a swollen turd.

I walk back to the tent. When I get there the three of them are still sleeping. I try to sleep too but the snores keep me awake. I count from 0 to 7,348.

The line of cars drags slowly and the air conditioning doesn't work. We listen three times — back to back — to a mix of Brazilian carnival music and two hours after we left we finally make it to the house.

Later in the evening Patricio and Seba come back home stumbling and singing while we're having dinner. Patricio's nose is bleeding and he's slurring and can't explain what happened. Seba says something about a bus driver Patricio might have called a 'wanker' and the bus driver beating him up, but he can't be sure and Patricio just keeps saying, 'It was so cool, man,' over and over. Until Carlos bangs his palms against the table, gets up, lifts Patricio by the collar of his polo shirt and shakes him several times so that a lighter, roll-up cigarettes and other things fall from his pockets. Patricio starts laughing and keeps laughing while Carlos slaps him around several times, back and forth. Alicia starts to cry and shouts something incomprehensible. Seba just looks like an idiot. The four of them rush upstairs and they keep shouting.

Until a plane cuts the screen from right to left, spinning around its axis, and a boat explodes several times.

The voice says these planes could fly very low, so low that radars wouldn't detect them. The voice also says the aviation played a heroic part during 'their baptism of fire, many times paying the ultimate price with honour and courage'. Then they play the national anthem. And then some dark-haired guys with snot and mud on their faces surrender to some soldiers who are all blond, shaven and clean. It's the same every year, although this year it happens two or three months earlier than usual. They must have run out of films. Nico gets up and changes channels.

A giant turtle with fluorescent green eyes swims towards us.

I remember this film, I remember watching it two or three years ago. There was a beautiful brunette mermaid called Jennie. And Apollo Creed was there too although he wasn't a boxer. And there was something about making a deal with the devil and never dying and never-ending love. And many other things I can't recall.

Alicia comes to the kitchen to get a glass of wine from the fridge. She tells us to turn the telly off and go to sleep.

The screen fades to black as two children carve their names on the back of a turtle, the same turtle when it was normal size, before it turned into a monster, before its eyes became fluorescent and green, before it ate Apollo Creed.

Early in the morning I go downstairs for a glass of water or I dream that I do. On the way back I spot or dream that I spot the door that leads to Helga's room half-open. I peer or dream that I peer inside: the bed is unmade and Alicia's slippers are lying on the floor, one on top of the other.

The sun pierces through the blinds, falling in streams, dripping all over the floor, the bed, the shelves, the walls. There's a desk full of picture frames: Helga in profile and in full colour; Helga wearing a mask at some party; Helga at her First Communion (a different angle from the picture downstairs); Helga at the seaside with an old couple — the man looks like Carlos but older; Helga with a Pekingese dog; Helga during her first year at school; Helga during her second year at school; Helga during her third year at school; Helga during her fourth year at school; Helga during her fifth year at school. A picture of the five of them next to a Mickey Mouse statue and another statue of a guy who looks like someone's uncle. A picture of the five of them wearing skiing clothes. A picture of the five of them in the dunes round the back of the house. A picture of Alicia, a young and happy and tired Alicia, holding Helga, a baby. There are teddies on the bed. Books on the shelves. Pens and pencils in a glass.

I go back or I dream that I go back to bed.

I wake up with Nico banging my head with a pillow. We go downstairs, toast some bread and eat while watching a German game show.

A man in lederhosen falls into pink water. Other accidents happen. People laugh. One of the teams wins.

Then we go to the dunes and catch a couple arriving on a motorbike. They hide the bike behind a bush and put a mat on the sand and soon they're kissing and touching and he goes on top and starts rubbing himself against her. I start laughing, Nico starts laughing too and we whistle and shout at them, and they get up, arrange their clothes, and look in all directions as we run back to the house with Nico limping at fast speed.

Six or seven monsters walk across a mountain as we eat biscuits with chocolate milk.

Big birds with horrible beaks; many of their feathers are missing and they're pretty boring. We change channels and are about to start watching a film called *The Towering Inferno* that, for some reason, promises tits, when the car parks in the garage: Carlos is back from the bus terminal, from sending Patricio, Seba and Alicia back to Rosario. He says we'll pack up tonight and leave tomorrow. He grabs a bottle of beer and goes upstairs and locks himself in his room. He leaves the wallet, the cigarettes, and the car keys on the table. Nico steals money from the wallet and we escape, on the bikes, to the arcade near the gas station. Nico pedals with one foot — we take forever but eventually get there.

He pays for the tokens. We spend at least two hours playing *Wonder Boy* and then fight over who'll break the record at *Space Harrier*. Nico goes first.

Bubbles leave the gun and kill all sorts of creatures — it's beautiful.

He plays three games in a row, always losing with the first monster. My turn comes and I make it to round two and then three. It's my moment of glory, perhaps the best moment in my life, and I'm about to make it to round four when the screen turns dark. I curse Nico for shutting the machine off but he swears he didn't touch anything. We shout at one another for a while but soon realise that all the machines are down. Without the fans the air inside becomes unbreathable and we walk out to the sidewalk. The gas station must have lost power too, because all the guys that are normally playing cards in the bar are now standing outside, smoking by the signs that warn against smoking there.

We sit near the bicycle rack and make a puddle of spit and sunflower-seed shells at our feet. We stay there at least for another hour, until it starts to get dark.

Back in the house Carlos is getting the fire ready, drinking beer straight from a one-litre bottle that drips condensation — the burning charcoal hisses with every drop. 'I'll grill the rest of the flank steak,' he says, and also the ribs — 'no one knows when the power will be back' and he doesn't want the meat to go off and in any case, we're leaving in the morning, we were always supposed to leave in the morning, we can take the cooked meat with us. He doesn't mention the money and he doesn't ask where we've been. He just drinks from his beer, moving the charcoal in silence, alternating his eyes between the fire and some point past the tennis court.

By the time the fire is ready it's already night; Carlos throws the meat on the grill and the air fills with smoke and the smell of burning beef. Then he lights the kerosene lamp and we eat in the garden, trying to keep the mosquitoes and the flies and all kinds of bugs away from the food, the Coke, the wine, and us. Carlos mentions something about buying a new road map and getting the oil checked before we leave. He also starts saying something about this summer and the summer last year but suddenly goes silent and pours himself another glass of wine.

When we're done, he turns the lamp off and we walk to the end of the garden and sit on a bench next to the empty swimming pool to watch the stars and the moon, to listen to the sound of the sea crashing against the rocks below.

We stay there, in silence, forever. Until a breeze springs up and the summer is over.

NOTES TOWARDS A RETURN

A note (unedited, in English).

Buenos Aires. 20.12.2016. A return — this seems to be one of the things I'm expected to write about. And now that I return, now that I find myself here, I haven't even left the airport and I'm already toying with the idea of writing a return, perhaps just to surrender, to stop running away from that mandate. To write about a return to a hot place, by a fictional character, broken by (self-)exile and memories. But how could this return be any different? What could this writerly return add to this well-trodden path? People — broken by (self-)exile and memories — have been returning to hot places, for an audience, since Ulysses (the first one?). And it's a terrible destiny, to find oneself in the mouth of a lyrical poet. This is very likely the most dangerous part of returning, that poetic possibility, the dangerous and fake nostalgia all poetry entails.

Missing Buenos Aires is a daily routine. Some days the longing arrives after a sound — memories are triggered, homesickness kicks in. Other times it happens after a smell, any smell, heavenly or foul. Most times the longing comes after the wanton recollection of this or that corner, any part of Buenos Aires that in my mind looks like how Buenos Aires should look. Some days the feeling is overwhelming and I can spend hours wallowing in self-pity. Most times the situation is manageable. I'm writing this, listening to Astor Piazzolla, because today is one of those days where I can't handle homesickness very well. The music helps with the fantasy, it feeds it.

Because the thing is: I never lived in Buenos Aires. I frequented Buenos Aires a lot, but I never lived there, never managed to settle there, had my name on a bill, or a fixed abode, or a favourite café that wasn't a cliché, or a library card. Unlike Dublin, Paris, and later London, Buenos Aires was too much for me — I couldn't tame it, own it, call it my own. I used to spend many a weekend in Buenos Aires but I would spend this time couch surfing, mostly off my head after rock concerts, preparing a landing that never materialised. So I miss the possibility of Buenos Aires. And by missing its possibility I can miss my own hometown without the uncomfortable bits, without all the impossibilities, the proximities, the complexities and familiarities. The parts that can hurt.

I miss an imaginary Buenos Aires instead of a real Rosario. Homesickness is safer this way. And besides, like this I can plug into some universal motifs of Argentineanness — perpetuated by literature, tango, film (Argentine and international) — that I no longer wish to contest, since I have long given up trying to express the nuances and the complications of being an Argentinean.

Of course I miss Buenos Aires.

Of course I play football.

Of course I'm a gifted tango dancer.

Of course I'm a charming Lothario.

Of course I'm prone to fits of passion and — unlike British guys — fits of tears.

Of course I can ride a horse.

Of course I'm a streetwise intellectual who likes to sit in cafés to solve the problems of the world.

I have, during these past fifteen years away from the possibility of Buenos Aires, become a simplified version of myself. My life is better without corners. And more importantly, in (self-)exile I have become what I always wanted to be: the stereotypical porteño.

I miss Buenos Aires. How could I not write about this now that I'm here, now that I return to the city I never left, the city where I never lived?

Ariel Ruzzo, Professor of Latin American Literature in some college, University of London, arrives in Buenos Aires after a hiatus of five years. Actually, make it Professor of Comparative Literature, it will be easier to market. And Comparative Literature sounds less of a con. It sounds like he went abroad to do the vini, vidi, vici. Professor of Latin American Literature, for an Argentine character like Ariel, sounds like he escaped an economic crisis to then accidentally find his way into a claustrophobic department, where he ended up teaching unsuspecting and overpaying students the soporific drivel known as magical realism.

So Ariel Ruzzo — Professor of Comparative Literature — lands in Buenos Aires after a hiatus of five years. He has come to sell a flat, a flat he inherited a while ago from an auntie, a flat in which he barely lived back in the late 1990s. He has found an overseas buyer, so it is only a matter of signing a couple of papers at the notary's, some other papers at the solicitors, receiving the money in his British account, and then back to London, to his office overlooking a square once frequented by Virginia Woolf.

But there is also the thing with the boxes: he has to remove some boxes from his flat. Rita, an ex-girlfriend, has been living there all this time, paying a symbolic rent, keeping the place alive. He would much rather avoid this, for a series of reasons, but he has already arranged to meet her tonight, have dinner together, old friends and all that, get the boxes out of the small storage corner under the stairs tomorrow. There must be five or six of them, said Rita. It can't take him that long — most will go in the bin anyway.

I don't remember where I was or why I was searching for images of Buenos Aires — it might have been a moment of procrastination; it could have been research towards an essay; it could have been anything. The reason for my search is no more but I remember very well the words, scribbled on a wall in some porteño suburb, in blue: 'morirse no es nada, peor es vivir en Argentina' — 'dying is meaningless, worse is living in Argentina'.

These words pin down very well the atmosphere of the 1990s and early 2000s — my 1990s and 2000s. The decade felt like a slow death, punctuated by a long series of socio-political and economic upheavals. Like many others, this slow death — peaking with the crash of 2001 — sent me away. In my particular case, away from the possibility of Buenos Aires, on a journey to become Argentinean. No, I don't know what I was before; I only know that I became Argentinean abroad, probably while I was cleaning a toilet in Dublin, and the toilet was full to the rim with shit. This was a defining moment in my life. The realisation must have hit me then and there, or during the series of crap jobs I had for years on end. Somehow, suddenly, it was clear: who I was, where I was from, what I could aspire to. It was both humbling and enlightening.

I know Ariel Ruzzo left for the same reasons, even if he likes to play the scholarly card. But I still wonder if he became Argentinean abroad. Is it a generalised disease, this displaced becoming? What was his 'cleaning an overflowing toilet' moment, if he ever had one?

Ariel has had a stellar career. From his undergraduate studies in Buenos Aires' School of Filosofía y Letras, to an MA in Cambridge, to a PhD in Princeton. A stellar career, from the very start, in all the right places. His thesis, which surveys the detective story from its birth in the mid-nineteenth century all the way to cinema noir (briefly touching on the work of Ricardo Piglia, a nice nationalistic gesture), has become one of those rare documents that manage to leap outside of the reduced spaces of academia, in order to become a non-fiction classic. *Reading the Detectives* is into its sixth edition and in the process of being translated into French and Japanese. And Ariel is only forty.

And yet, success aside, here is Ariel, back in Buenos Aires, like any mortal, after a hiatus of five years, and even before getting off the plane it is clear that it will be a difficult trip, that coming back to Argentina always involves a process of re-adaptation and submission. There is a transport strike and among the people exercising their right to piss off everyone else we should count those in charge of driving Ariel and his fellow passengers from the plane to the airport. And no, the captain won't let them walk the scant hundred metres to the terminal, because it contravenes a series of safety regulations, even if passengers from other planes seem to be able to do the walk. A two-hour wait, then, until British Airways manages to find a scab to do the job, in several trips, old people and those with kids first, no mention of literature professors.

Ariel is back in Buenos Aires, after a hiatus of five years. He will have to come back later to get his suitcase — the strike — or get a courier to pick it up on his behalf. But he's back.

But I should be taking notes, there are so many things to remember, so many things that could go into that piece about a return, things that add realism, the details, the lived feeling. Now that I find myself in Buenos Aires I should be noting things down, focusing on the contradictory bits, because readers love the contradictory bits, not only of returns.

In the subte, Línea B, between Gallardo and Medrano: a mother with a disabled kid. She's having a loud go at him when he tries to eat a cookie and the crumbs fall all over the place, as he contorts visibly in pain with some muscular malfunction. The mother, tired, aged prematurely — she resents the child, not that I have to guess this, because she says, 'I can't stand you anymore,' in Spanish obviously. And then she realises she needs to get off, and makes her move, politely asking the other passengers in the carriage to make room for her and the wheelchair-bound kid, all charm. This must be the first time in my life I hear a porteño say sorry, please, thank you. I'm impressed.

This is a world apart from my first experience of Buenos Aires on my own, in 1995 or 1996. I was walking down the avenue connecting the Retiro bus terminal with the city centre — it was an ocean of people. I was a bleary-eyed lad coming to the smoke from a place where we swallowed the S's at the end of the words — El interior but not even really El interior, nothing that endearing or worthy of a story by Saer. Still, I was bleary-eyed and scared and walking maybe too slowly and maybe on the wrong side of the pavement. A redhead guy suddenly turned up before me, kindly shouted in my face that I kindly move aside and pushed me aside, kindly. I almost fell kindly on the floor but I didn't.

I wonder if this kind redhead is now as polite as the mother on the subte.

The car flies down the Ricchieri. Thank god the driver is quiet and Ariel can dedicate his time to watching the ugly houses on both sides of the highway, sprouting like verrucas. Many an Argentine house built since the big migration waves of the early Twentieth century is an example of Feísmo, the

Modernism and beyond of the impoverished European, at home and abroad, he reminds himself, almost as if he were thinking in footnotes. Who lives here? What is it like to live by the side of this road that never sleeps, with planes over your head, in one of these eyesores?

He's about to find a provisional answer to this question when the love motels catch his attention. He might have gone to all of them, here on the outskirts of civilisation. What a perfect site for love motels. A perfect place to stop for a shag before you make it to Buenos Aires and get lovelessly screwed by the city. He once was in one of these love hotels — or he imagines he was in one, or I imagine he was in one, which for a fiction piece would be the same — called París. He might have gone there with Rita, before he got the flat, when the options were shagging against a tree or in a rented room, shifts of two hours, mirror on the ceiling, adult channel not included in the standard rate. They might have gone to a room called La Torre. There might have been a photo of the Eiffel Tower glued to the window, both blocking potential perverts from peering in from the parking lot and providing the ambience. Or, like I said, he could have imagined all this, or I could have, thinking about his ghosts, planning his return in my head.

But it doesn't matter who imagined or imagines this — soon Buenos Aires is there, to the right and to the left, tower blocks, barrios, more lack of planning, advertisement hoardings that look like soft porn, seen from the elevated Avenida de Mayo. And a song starts playing on the radio, make it a tango, make it Piazzolla, make it legible and easy for foreign audiences, the ones likely to read this piece about a return.

And the poor, their dark faces underground — it's always a matter of skin, whatever Argentineans might tell you. The pregnant woman with several children, begging barefoot in Pueyrredón, when I get off to change to the line that will take me to Once station, where I have to catch a suburban train to Ituizangó. The kids' dirty faces, their shredded clothes. They might be the same poor kids I see later on the train — poor but with air conditioning. Poor but spoiled after the tragedy of Once in 2012, when fifty-one died crushed like sardines when the 3772 from Moreno decided to enter the station at full speed. I can't guarantee trains are able to stop now, but at least they have aircon.

These kids or other kids, around eleven or twelve years old, drinking warm white wine from a plastic bottle, happy and off the trolley. And the itinerant salesmen offering everything from sweets and colouring books to a CD with the latest hits of x radio — they are playing the songs with a contemporary ghetto blaster, the salesman showing off a voice probably acquired during a journalism degree. And the Africans. Africans in Buenos Aires — they're back. Speaking a language I can't pin down, sitting in groups of two or three, ignored by the other passengers, for better or worse, travelling to provincia with bags and suitcases. What are they doing here? Where are they going? There used to be many of them in Buenos Aires but then they vanished — blended into the white population over the years, according to some; decimated by the flu and the war with Paraguay, according to the ones who know better. And now they are back. Like ghosts. Is there any other way of being back other than as a ghost?

Ariel uses his keys and comes in unannounced. The door is heavy. He remembers the door being heavy but it must have gotten heavier during these past five years.

Soon he's riding the lift all the way to the sixth floor. It's an old Otis with scissor gates. He thought they had been banned — children kept getting their hands and feet crushed by the gates. But here is this lift with scissor gates and it feels like being in a film, cinematically moving up with the numbers of the floors painted on the walls turning up one after the other and this irregular chiaroscuro of shadows and lights, scrolling in vertical pans.

And soon the sixth floor. Ariel leaves the lift, closes the scissor gates behind him, and the lift disappears towards the ground floor, called by another person. The door to his flat opens and Rita is there, unwilling to be taken by surprise. She looks beautiful, the same, she hasn't aged a single minute. Or maybe he never paid attention.

The dead. If I were to write that piece about a return, of Ariel's return, I should make a reference to the dead of Buenos Aires. The dead might explain the ghosts, or add some material basis for them, or just some colour.

The dead of Buenos Aires, underground. Not as in buried six feet under but given a platform in the actual metro stations, on station names and writing on walls — the battles, violent patriarchs, terrorist attacks, catastrophes, accidents, disappeared writers. Caseros — Ejército Grande versus Juan

Manuel de Rosas (another station and one more tyrant we love to hate) 1852. Pasteur / AMIA — vaccination / suicide bombing. Carlos Gardel — plane crash, Medellín, 1935. Rodolfo Walsh — killed in Constitución, 1977, disappeared. But maybe I'm exaggerating, forcing wanton connections. Or maybe not, because Cromañón.

By the tracks, in the depths, a small mural consecrated to the dead in the fire of Cromañón, where almost two hundred music fans burned to a cinder during a rock concert, in 2004. The choice of words in the mural, on the black wall, links to other deaths: 'Cromañón Nunca más'. Nunca más; Never More. The words chosen back in the mid-'80s to attempt to quantify and qualify the crimes of the juntas between 1976 and 1983. *Nunca más* was the title of the book by the National Commission on the Disappearance of Persons, two words that would also become a call to stop death. In the mid-'80s the call was to stop state terrorism. In the early 2000s a call to stop another type of death: one born out of the state's disappearance, all the corruption and oversights that would make it possible for almost two hundred — many of whom were children — to die in a blaze.

A piece about a return to Buenos Aires wouldn't be a piece about a return to Buenos Aires without some paragraphs dedicated to the dead. This is, of course, another trope I'm expected to write about, another form of surrender, part of the demand that Argentine writers fill the page looking back towards this or that violent past. Disappeared, victims of terrorism or petty crime, any of these will do to please the reader. Perhaps the dead might grant me the attention of a publisher too. Perhaps I have to be that opportunistic, like many of my successful compatriots. Maybe just once.

And of course they have fucked by now. Ariel is smoking a cigarette, lying in his estranged bed. Rita is smoking too. Of course they are smoking.

And of course a dialogue will here ensue, one of those dialogues full of love, longing and bitterness. Like Graciela Dufau and Héctor Alterio talking while promenading by the rotten Riachuelo in a 1982 film about another return, *Volver*, unimaginatively named after the tango tune with the same name.

Alfredo (Alterio) comes back to Argentina, tortured by (self-)exile. He comes back for work, although not only for work. He's a successful businessman in the USA, and he comes back to Buenos Aires, in 1982, when the dictatorship is crumbling, and the Malvinas stupidity is about to happen. He returns, and he works and he beds Beatriz (Dufau), an old flame. And then — or even before they get laid, I can't remember and I don't wish to watch this film again — they are walking by the Riachuelo, in a clichéd postcard spot better avoided, yet abused by art, cinema, music and literature. There are still dock workers here and there, because they had not yet been decimated by neoliberalism. Alfredo and Beatriz walk, loving and hating one another in dub, in sepia, with corny phrases, so much to say, in so little time. And of course Beatriz is a journalist, just like Rita, who starts speaking over the dialogue in *Volver*, perhaps reading my mind or Ariel's, or perhaps to stop me from reproducing the original exchange of platitudes.

'Why did you come?' asks Rita.

'To sell the flat, you know that,' says Ariel. 'And to see Buenos Aires.'

'I mean why did you really come? You didn't really need to.'

'I was curious.'

'Tourists,' says Rita bitterly. 'In just a few days they want to see everything: visit all the museums, watch the tango, the football. Everything. As long as it is authentic.'

'And I really wanted to see you,' says Ariel. 'I've missed you.'

'Have you realised how much we sound like characters in a bad Argentine film?' asks Rita.

'It's the fate of all Argentine characters,' says Ariel and lights up another cigarette. Or I might say that. But he definitely lights up a cigarette because I quit smoking years ago.

And the dead of the AMIA, murdered in the terror attack of 1994. How many of them? Was it eighty-five of them? The names are painted on the walls at Pasteur / AMIA — white traces against a black wall, also underground. I don't count them.

The ideologues behind the attack were never found. The investigation pointed towards a cocktail of Islamist terrorism, state and police complicity, inefficiency, and old-school Argentine antisemitism. There was an Iranian connection and years of nothing and then a national prosecutor in charge of the investigation. He was found dead twenty and so years later, in January 2015, a day before declaring in front of Congress, in a move that according to some would have compromised the then-president Cristina Kirchner (who had recently signed a controversial deal with Iran in order to advance the investigation, if you ask some; in order to shelve it, if you ask others). As his death was investigated things started to turn up about him, dirty laundry. Inappropriate exchanges of information with the American embassy in Buenos Aires, bank accounts abroad, links to foreign secret services. No one will ever know who suicided him. As it is very likely that no one will ever know who bombed the AMIA in 1994, or the Israeli embassy some blocks away, two years earlier. Justice is so slow in Argentina, that frequently it never arrives.

I can't remember if it was after the attack on the embassy or the AMIA, when an outraged and emotional old lady on the telly, reflecting upon the atrocity, ended her speech with 'why do they have to put a bomb here? They haven't only killed Jews today, they have also killed Argentine people, innocent people.'

All this would make interesting material.

Ariel spends the night with Rita. The next morning he goes for a walk.

If the piece had taken place during the '80s, Ariel sooner or later would have bumped into a disappeared-theme demo. If it had taken place in the 1990s, he would have bumped into one against the political corruption and the economic misery that characterised the decade. In 2001 he would have bumped into a horde of angry citizens demanding that all politicians go — que se vayan todos. In the past fifteen years he would have bumped into demos for or against the populist saints or sinners who saved or destroyed the country, that bunch of holy crooks, the Kirchners — Argentina is a country of radical binaries, don't ask me to explain this in this limited space, in a piece of fiction.

And now, after hanging around Florida and Lavalle, Ariel is walking down Carlos Pellegrini heading towards Corrientes, being the tourist that he is, when he bumps into a demo, pure coincidence. The posters betray the same lack of imagination as in any demo anywhere. The semiotics of red and black, block capitals, synthetic slogans. A large flag with Che's face confirms that the lack of imagination in this opportunity is left-leaning. And here a closer look at the posters and signs: they don't make any sense. Ariel feels dizzy but nevertheless starts to walk with the demonstrators, gets in the midst of the noise, unable to understand the language they speak (metaphorically) and he crosses Avenida 9 de Julio with them, and then stops and watches them disappear banging their drums and singing their chants against the traffic down Corrientes, with that obscene erected Obelisk behind him, and a giant mural of Evita watching him from the building of the Ministerio de Obras Públicas.

He watches them disappear. Unable to process what is going on, what do they want, what is it about now? He can't understand because he has spent five years away, because he has slowly disengaged himself from his country, because he doesn't belong here anymore — Rita is right: he's a tourist. And yet he's already thinking of a possible conference paper, why not a journal article: 'Peripatetic Literature: Argentine Politics and the Poetics of the Demo'. The title just turns up in his mind. He doesn't even need to know what the demo was about in order to write this. The reason can be found out later, or just invented. He only needs to know that the demo happened. That it will happen again. That Argentines love a demo. And that demos are just another form of literature.

And that all literature can and should be captured, killed and vivisected.

I spend two weeks in Buenos Aires and never make it home, to the place where I was born and where I spent twenty-five years of my life. Let's just say that a number of personal and work-related commitments impede it. I get to see my family, most of them. But I don't see my friends, except for the ones who have turned the possibility of Buenos Aires into a reality. A natural order is repaired by my inability to bridge the 350 kilometres that separate me from Rosario. Some friends verbalise their disappointment and I stop responding to their messages. Others stop replying to my fake apologies. The important part is that a heavy ballast is dropped: we should have stopped talking years ago — we have nothing in common anymore — we were victims of the Dictatorship of Nostalgia that comes with social media.

I spend two weeks in Buenos Aires, tying up projects, meeting this or that writer or filmmaker, sorting out papers, buying books and films and eating meat and drinking wine. Working but not only working but also having a reason to be here, for once. And taking down notes — I take down lots of notes, in my notebook. Obviously I take notes with a fountain pen, on a small Moleskine — this is part of my process of simplification, of embracing the stereotype, even the stereotypes I have invented for myself, in other writerly fantasies.

I take notes in bars, on the bus, on the train and the subte. And people peer at my notes but the notes are in English.

A girl on the train speaks to me (in English) after eyeing my writing, 'Where are you from?' she says, with my same accent. I reply to her in Spanish. She seems disappointed and asks why I write in English then. I reply that I don't know. She laughs. She's beautiful and young, and gets off at the next station, Villa Luro. This girl was some moments ago sitting zazen on the train floor. I had never seen anyone sitting zazen in Buenos Aires. It's never all about poverty or misery, is it? Not even when I think for an audience, for the page, speculatively, erasing the complexities and colours, in order to please, to be synthetic and available, to be nice to my reader.

At some point I start missing London. I count the days. Thank god the days fly. I can live a different lie there, one that feels real.

After one more session of love with Rita, more tender than passionate, and very likely sterile, hopefully, Ariel sets to the task of getting the boxes out from their hideout.

What he finds will colour the nature of his return, whatever else happens before or after. Perhaps he finds notes. Or notebooks. Yes, notebooks of his years as a porteño intellectual, the years before the Big Leap into other continents and into a properly structured way of life, a career. Or maybe he finds nothing of any significance. The thought makes him anxious.

He does open the boxes. The first two house old books eaten away by damp and cockroaches (do they eat books?). He moves these aside, keeps opening. Old clothes, old readers from his undergraduate years. Everything ready for the skip, smelling of time and death.

But the smell of coffee soon starts to fill the flat, the melancholia is aborted, and Rita turns up with a cup, wearing a long white shirt, barefoot, all post-coital happiness. She moves next to Ariel, crouches next to him, passes him the cup, kisses him on the cheek.

'It's all rotten,' he says, Ariel, opening another box.

'It's very humid down there,' says Rita; she sits on the floor, careful that the T-shirt clothes what some minutes ago was in the open, because this is how old friends sleep together.

Paper, this is all paper, and yes, he finally gets to the notebooks. He had the foresight of wrapping them in cling film. They seem unharmed. Two notebooks, pseudo-Moleskine, national production, they will fall apart as soon as the cling film is removed. He moves them to a side, doesn't bother with them, not now.

'All this can go in the bin,' he says, pointing at the rest of the boxes, the six stinking boxes, with their mouths open towards the ceiling.

'Polo,' says Rita, referring to the building doorman, 'he can sort this out when he clears the rest of the rubbish tomorrow night, after I leave.'

'Is Polito still alive?' asks Ariel, surprised.

'Yes!' says Rita.

'I'd love to say hi to him,' he says. He won't.

I'm waiting in the departures lounge, Ezeiza airport. I tell myself that I will be back before the end of the year, that this time I'll make the effort to go back home, not to an ideal or imaginary place, but to the only place I really left behind, to whoever still speaks to me there, to my mother's house, my childhood things, the books I wish I hadn't read, the places where I used to spend my time. Of course I won't.

But they have Wi-Fi in the airport now and it works quite well. I play with my phone, read the news in English, respond to banal messages (only the banal ones), and when I run out of battery I look at the passing people, singling out the Argentines without effort, their familiar ways and blue jeans and gigantic Nike trainers sticking out in the flurry of wealthy Brazilian tourists, mugged Europeans on their way home, and air hostesses and pilots with their small suitcases rolling over linoleum floors.

I sit here, listening to the repetitive muzak, waiting to fly back to London, and I think about Ariel's return, about how the rest of his journey might unfold for him.

In the next days, after relocating to an AirBnB flat in Palermo Hollywood, he will dedicate himself full-time to sorting out the final details of the sale. Rita will be too busy, organising her move first and settling into her new place later, to meet him until the very last moment. He will welcome this space, spend his time in the bookshops of Calle Corrientes, the bars, perhaps even go watch a film in one of the old cinemas left down Calle Lavalle, if they haven't all turned into evangelic temples. He will end up signing the papers by the end of the week and receive the confirmation of the bank transfer the following Monday morning. The notebooks will remain unopened until after the sale, the transfer, after all the to-dos, and Rita. Until he's had time to breathe and properly realise that he has nothing left in

Buenos Aires, that all his traces in this place are contained in these two notebooks. So he leaves it until this very last moment, when I'm sitting at the departures lounge in Ezeiza airport, waiting for the plane that will take me to London, to the place we call home.

The cling film comes off easily and the notebooks don't fall apart. The first one — a clutter of blue and black ink — contains mostly quotes from this or that book. The second one, this is the one that matters. The first page makes it clear.

A note (unedited, in Spanish).

Ezeiza airport, April 13, 2002. A departure. This seems to be one of the tropes I'm expected to write about. And now that I depart, now that I'm here waiting for the plane that will take me away, I toy with the idea of writing something about a departure, perhaps just to surrender, to stop running away from this mandate, or from the fact that I'm leaving. I'M LEAVING. And I don't have a clue what will happen with my life, where I'll end up, doing what. It's such a cliché, for an Argentinean to depart, and to write about it. It's a terrible destiny; it reeks so much of tango. But at least it's something to do. And what's more: departing is meaningless; worse is living in Argentina.

AcKNoWLedGEMeNTS

Of all the myths surrounding literature none is further from the truth than fancying the journey of the writer as a solitary and heroic quest. But that it is impossible to survive the blank page alone is obvious to anyone approaching it armed with a second language. There were many sidekicks instrumental in turning this book into a reality — here is a very likely incomplete attempt to nod at them.

Without the constant learning that is editing a literary journal none of these stories would have made it to the page. My thanks to everyone involved in the *Minor Literature[s]* cargo cult — whether you are an editor, a contributor, or a reader, our conversations, agreements and disagreements are central to my cerebral activity.

Earlier versions of some of these stories appeared in *3:AM Magazine*, *Numéro Cinq* and *Open Pen* — many thanks to the editors who saw value in them. Some of these stories were also published in the USA by LCG Media — my thanks for their input and support. Needless to say that this book wouldn't be in your hands now without the labour of love that is Influx Press — to them, my enduring gratitude. To all of the above: please, keep taking risks.

This book is in many ways a response to other stories, films, music, and art, from different places, thrown together here in order to concoct a constellation that might make sense of this disjointed existence I have written myself into. The constellation hasn't joined any pieces together but I trust the references in the book are clear enough to avoid turning these final paragraphs into a redundant name-dropping exercise.

So finally, family and friends: you already know what there is to be known. But in the unlikely event you read this book and reach this page: thanks for the love and patience and sorry for the time these stories stole from us. Nevertheless, I can think of many worse things than turning lost time into books.

ABOUT THE AUTHOR

Fernando Sdrigotti was born in Rosario (Argentina) in 1977. His fiction and critical writing has appeared widely online and in print, and has been translated into French, Italian, Turkish, Norwegian and Spanish. *Shitstorm,* a novella, was published in 2018 by Open Pen. *Dysfunctional Males,* his first collection of short stories in English, was published in 2017 by LCG Media. He lives in London.